SCREAMS FROM THE BAYOU

A HORROR ANTHOLOGY

Foreword by Jonathan Janz

Edited by Heather Ann Larson

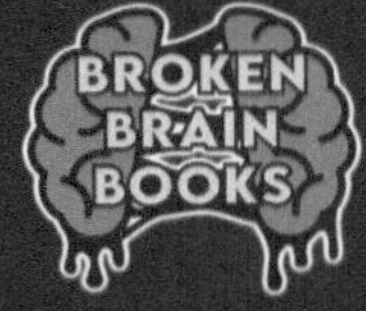

SWAMP DIRECTORY

Screams from the Bayou and the Delicious Terror of Southern Gothic Stories

An Introduction by Jonathan Janz

At some point this summer, I got asked to write the introduction to an anthology of short stories. Because my schedule was already too packed, I almost said no. But two factors prevented me from declining. One was that I knew several writers in the anthology, and I knew they had serious game; the other was that I have a soft spot for Southern Gothic literature.

Oh, who am I kidding? When it's done well, I

love Southern Gothic stories. My first experience with the genre was Faulkner's LIGHT IN AUGUST, though Flannery O'Connor's sublime "A Good Man Is Hard to Find" was definitely one that imprinted on me early as well. Those tales broke the rules. They *went there*. Even in the sweltering heat of a summer's day, even under the blinding eye of a pitiless midafternoon sun, the most terrible things could happen (or to paraphrase Peter Straub, the most *dreadful* things). In Southern Gothic literature, I soon learned, daylight and warmth didn't mean safety. In fact, they seemed to amplify the horrors that erupted even in the most mundane of situations. And at night...

At night the perils of the South were even worse.

Southern Gothic literature doesn't have to be horror, but it certainly has a rich tradition in the horror genre. Just a few of my favorites include...

The Elementals & *Blackwater* by Michael McDowell
A Feast of Snakes by Harry Crews
All the Sinners Bleed by S.A. Cosby
"A Good Man Is Hard to Find" by Flannery O'Connor
The Bottoms & *Cold in July* by Joe R. Lansdale
A Killing Fire & *A Killing Rain* by Faye Snowden
Sharp Objects by Gillian Flynn
Fevre Dream by George R.R. Martin
The Reformatory & *Ghost Summer* by Tananarive Due
As I Lay Dying & *Sanctuary* by William Faulkner
Blood Meridian & *Child of God* by Cormac McCarthy
Interview with the Vampire by Anne Rice
Tobacco Road & *God's Little Acre* by Erskine Caldwell

Perusing the above titles, I can see that they're wildly varied, yet if I'm scouring for commonalities, here are some I encounter again and again:

--A powerful sense of place and atmosphere. The setting of a Southern Gothic is every bit as important as the setting of a sci-fi novel or fantasy series.

--Dark secrets, the kind that make you shudder in the small hours of the night.

--The existence of evil and goodness, though not always in equal measure. Southern Gothic features the kind of malevolence you wish didn't exist and the kind of nobility that makes you happy you're alive.

--The horrors of racism, the generational pain it inflicts, and the consequences that occur when communities let it flourish and fester.

--The unique isolation, both physical and emotional, that can occur in the forest, the swamp, or even a lake house where the murky waters conceal unspeakable things.

--The consuming nature of sin, often lust and greed, and the downward drag those elements exert on the soul.

So I suppose when I agreed to write the introduction to this anthology, the reader in me wanted to explore some of the above elements and themes, to return to the South and dwell in its torrid heat, and to reside in a place where escape is well-nigh impossible. I wanted to *live* in the bayou for a while, skulk through its shadowlands, and spend a few evenings as a voyeur to characters who'd reveal their secret lives, no matter how sinister or unnerving.

If you've read this far, you're probably wondering one thing: Did these tales deliver?

Oh yes, my friend. Yes, they did.

Because these stories will...

...make you tap your feet to the music and tremble in the presence of the Swamp King.

...introduce you to a creature that will haunt your dreams and persuade you to stay the hell away from dark waters.

...chill you as a man and woman get caught in a storm...and soon learn what's *in* the storm.

...mesmerize you with the mysterious tale of a sisterhood whose bond is deeper than even the bloodiest wounds.

...chronicle a couple and what befalls them when they choose the worst possible night to leave the interstate for a bite to eat.

...spin a diabolical yarn of voodoo revenge featuring a fearsome woman and her two very loyal, very *frightening* friends.

...grip you in a stranglehold with a thrilling, twisty hunt for a killer named the Bayou Butcher.

...follow a trio of convicted felons as they're confronted with an unholy danger...one that *whispers*.

...unveil a bone-chilling creation called the Grunch, an individual guaranteed to make your flesh crawl.

...acquaint you with an awe-inspiring artifact possessed of a power that's as tantalizing as it is perilous.

...plunge you into a pulse-pounding nightmare about a child, his mother, and their mysterious neighbor.

...capture the loneliness and isolation of a new kid, as well as evoking the paralyzing fear induced by the entity the kid encounters.

...recruit you for a hunting expedition for a fabled creature, an expedition that becomes a fight for survival that's both shocking and visceral.

...invite you to a party, one with plenty of drinking, sultry encounters, and a most unwelcome visitor that will make you whimper in fear.

In other words, these tales will put you *through* it, but isn't that why you picked up this book? To experience Southern Gothic tales that make you sweat while they freeze your blood? To transport you to the bayou, a place where screams of terror are as frequent as they are futile? To give you teeth-chattering chills and make you happy you're nowhere near the swamp?

Speaking of chills...

As I sit here finishing this introduction this morning, it is twelve degrees in my part of Indiana, and most of the roads are impassable due to nearly ten inches of snowfall. It's blustery, icy, and white.

Yet because of these stories, my imagination is still dwelling in a place where it's warm and muggy, a place where the sweat runs down my skin in rivulets and every sound I hear is rife with mystery and danger. Despite the freezing grip of the winter storm outside my house, these tales are making the air I breathe soupy and hot, and ordinarily, I'd say that's a good thing. After all, I much prefer the warmth to the cold, and the bayou heat would almost certainly feel pleasant right about now.

But I wouldn't journey there even if I could. Because the bayou offers more than balmy weather. It provides a haven for fell creatures and deeds, mortal dangers human and otherwise. It's the kind of place I'd rather read about than visit, a kingdom of nightmares and unutterable deeds. And the book you're about to experience? It's your gateway to that kingdom.

So hunker with me here in the shadows. Because this is as far as I'll go.

See where I'm pointing? The place you're heading is right up there, through those cypress trees. Do you see the moonlight gleaming on the water? Do you hear the swamp sounds? Do you smell the decomposing life and the unwholesome stench of the bayou's otherworldly denizens?

Go ahead, friend. It's time for you to enter. Just don't expect to survive unscathed.

Because in the bayou, the monsters are real.

And they're eager for your company.

Bayou Boogie

Edmund Stone

The Blues roll on like molasses from a jar, smooth and thick, the notes sweet as anything, as I play tonight, like many a night out next to the edge of the bayou. I sit in this rundown, smoke-filled juke joint with a guitar in hand, playing songs to help people forget about their troubles. I try to lull them into a place of complacency away from the real world.

My name's Remi Martin, or The Blues Man from the Mississippi Delta, as most call me. Sometimes I think I'm more hype than legend, but then I could be wrong. I'll let you decide.

My stage is always set the way my daddy taught me, and his daddy before. It all came from when my great-granddaddy sang in the fields, picking cotton during Jim Crow days and before, when they was all enslaved to the plantation owners. To survive, they learned a certain magic, something like hoodoo or, like folks around here call, back-country voodoo.

The Blues I sing comes from the sorrow of the many, all working with one voice through songs. In perfect harmony, it wields a power like no one's ever heard. Over the years, my guitar, Betty, has listened to me sing it. When she helps me play, she has the power to sniff out the vilest and find a way to tame them. Sometimes, I think the soul of all those folks came before me is inside Betty, waiting to be released when needed. I believe this with all my heart. So when a couple of boys up to no good came into my club and start speaking about some treasure they know about, Betty is on guard.

Snitch and Carmichael, a couple of worthless fuckers if you ever seen any, start talking about the Swamp King and how he sings the blues better than anyone around. They say he would bet his treasure on it, one he has buried in the swamp.

"Remi," Snitch says, "I told that so and so he ain't ever going to outplay you. He said he wanted to try. I told him he ain't got nothing over you, Remi."

Normally I would agree with him, but I've heard about the Swamp King and his voodoo magic. It makes me wonder if he only said he could outplay me because he has a trick or two up his sleeve. Whatever the reason, he sent these two to tell me because I'm sure he wants a meeting.

Now, I play all around these bars and blues clubs from one end of the Delta to the other, going along the Gulf Shore and back into New Orleans, where the vampires walk among the crowds, looking for their next meal. I play them all, and I can see there are few who can match me, even the Swamp King.

I run my slide down the neck of Betty and stretch a few strings close to the end of the bridge, then I bring my hand back close to the top of the neck, stopping abruptly. "He say that, huh? What you all really think?"

"Oh no, Remi, we know you the best," Carmichael chimes in. "You beat everyone 'round these parts. Ain't no one any better."

"How 'bout you, Snitch? You believe my riffs are better than the Swamp King's?"

I spy the slightest hesitation on his face, as if he's searching for the right answer but not finding anything but confusion. I can tell he's considering the magic; it's always the magic.

"Well hell, Remi, I done told you. You's the best."

Chuckling at the strange way he says this, with little to no confidence on his face, I'm immediately set back. "Since we's all on the same page, I want to know why you really came in here. You come to make an offer, ain't you?"

"Just wait a minute, Remi," Carmichael says. "Don't you want to get some of that Swamp King treasure? I hear he's got a pretty good penny out there in that swamp, and he's just waiting for someone to challenge him for it. Don't you want to be the one to do it? We could split the money fifty-fifty."

Wickedly, I grin at the boys standing there, the expression of no understanding as absent as their teeth. If a challenge is being laid down, then I'm all ears. Except I thought the price a bit too steep.

"You want me to go to the swamp, it's gonna cost more than half."

Snitch turns to Carmichael and looks at him like I know they're up to no good. They smell like the swamp, making for a stench I don't like.

"What's your price?"

"You take me to the King and I win," ain't no doubt in my mind I would, "then I take seventy-five percent.

Unless you can do that, I ain't going nowhere."

They discuss my offer, moving their heads so close to each other I figure they'll crack skulls. The Swamp King I know has money, a treasure larger than anyone could imagine. He got it all during his time as a gangster, the most ruthless of them all.

Rumor has it his magic is very old, coming from a time when this area was unexplored. He's half Native and half African, mixed from the ancestors of both, a real bocor and very dangerous. They say he can conjure the dead on a whim.

I've also heard he has been shot up, the result of a heist gone wrong, his face all mangled and body not working properly. But I've learned, with the proper magic, it wouldn't matter much what he looks like; he could still be very formidable.

"Alright, Remi, we'll take your deal. Let's go tonight, after you're done here."

"Sure thing. I'll get warmed up and then we off for the swamp."

When we arrive in the middle of nowhere, next to a swamp on the edge of the bayou, a strange mojo enters my body. I can't shake the feeling I'm being set up, ambushed in a way, and the two who accompany me are walking me right into a trap. The need for solace weighs heavy on my mind, and sweat beads on my forehead as a result.

The humid night only adds to the discomfort. I'm thinkin' this is a bad idea and maybe I should just tell these fools to turn around and light out of here when I hear a noise come from down the way in the woods.

A loud groan, like someone in distress, sends my nerves to the edge of fight or flight, but Snitch and Carmichael are calm as cucumbers. It makes me think I'm right about these two and they're under the Swamp King's spell. I pat Betty, asking for her protection—it's all I can do.

A large, lumbering thing about ten feet tall comes for me out of the dark. Chills run down my back at the sight of it. It's mossy green from top to bottom, part human, or at least it looks like it had been once upon a time. Pieces of gray bone show like a half-opened package around its head, elbows, knees, and a little on its shoulders, but there's so much greenery there it's hard to see what's underneath. Dark sockets, deeper than the swamp water, show in place of eyes. Another long groan, and the thing I thought would eat us only leans forward, resting on its fists and overly large forearms, like some gorilla a person would see in the zoo.

"C'mon, ole Charoon is gonna take us to the King," Carmichael says.

I scrunch my face, trying to figure out how this is going to happen, when I see a small boat behind the creature, floating at the edge of the swamp water. Soon we're going along, with Charoon pulling us.

He's so big his feet touch bottom, the water only up to his chest at its deepest point. Gators move to the side, swimming away as fast as possible, with no interest in engaging Charoon in any way. A long rope made of dried vines braided together loops around his neck, but the monster doesn't protest. He goes along like it's his goal in life to transport people to their doom. My fear is he might be taking us to that very place.

An island appears ahead, with torch lights in the

middle, illuminating an area full of huts. Dried bones adorn the trees on the shore, connected by vines from the moss above, hanging like warning signs for those who enter to beware.

Charoon rises, producing a ripple in the water large enough to send the boat rocking. I hold to the sides, hoping the motion doesn't cause me to lose my supper. Stepping onto the ground, Charoon turns and pulls the rope and the boat onto the shore.

I step out first, onto the solid ground, holding the case Betty rests in tight against me. Snitch and Carmichael are next, and I find myself worrying. Satisfaction in the form of a smirk is plastered all over their faces, and I think I may have misjudged how stupid they really are.

This smells like a set up, but what can I do? Out here in the middle of nowhere, my only transportation back is a swamp monster who only takes orders from the Swamp King. It ain't my idea of security. I better be ready to play my heart out, as it's probably goin' to be my only way out of this.

I watch uncomfortably as Charoon eats a possum he picks up as it tries to scurry away. The crunch of bone and blood spurting from his mouth does nothing to reassure me of being in the right place.

"Hey, King, I brought him, just like I said I would," Snitch says.

Turning my head, I spy the Swamp King and can't believe what I'm seeing. A man in a wheelchair with half his face gone stares at me with one glass eye, the other sharp as a knife blade.

A couple of large goons are beside him, the looks on their faces like they're in a trance—the result of maybe enchantments the King put on them, I didn't know, but it makes sense, anyway.

Oddly, the Swamp King has a feeding tube that one of the goons holds, pouring some kind of clear liquor down it. One of the King's hands lays limply on his side, making me wonder how the man even picks up a guitar, or anything else for that matter. The Swamp King seems more of an enigma than anything set in reality.

Speaking in a raspy voice full of phlegm, the King addresses me. "So, you the man they call Remi? The one who plays the best blues this side of the Delta?"

"So's they say," I come back, my voice full of more bravado than I own.

"That so? Well, I hope you came to play that six string in your hand."

"If'n I do, do I get your treasure?"

The King laughs. "If you do, which is highly unlikely."

"If'n I don't?"

His eyes narrow, and he produces a grin slicker than the possum Charoon just ate. "You don't and I feed you to the gators."

I turn and give Snitch and Carmichael a stern look of disdain. These motherfuckers knew all along this could be a suicide mission and neglected to tell me. It don't matter, though, because I'm gonna outplay this fool and then we'll just see if those two assholes get any of the money.

I shrug, acting as though I'm unimpressed with the proposition, then notice there's no power to plug Betty into. "I'd love to play, but how am I supposed to electrify my guitar?"

The Swamp King laughs, then snaps his finger. The sharp sound is like a crack of thunder as lightning rolls across the sky, a bolt hitting a pole close by. Ripples of electricity roll across the ground, coming toward me. I jump back, and the bolt stops where I'm standing. My eyes widen when I see an electrical outlet protruding from the ground. It snaps and sparks like it's alive. One of the goons walks an amplifier over to the outlet and plugs it in, regarding me like I'm an ant standing below him.

Nervously, I kneel, setting the guitar case in front of me and opening it with trembling fingers. *C'mon, Betty, don't let me down*, I say, but I know deep down she won't. The girl has saved me many times in the past, so there's no reason to think she won't now.

Pulling the cord from within the case, I plug it into the port on the front of Betty and then take the other side and insert it into the amplifier. The box cracks and makes static sounds, then the old familiar hum resonates through Betty's pickups and I feel the energy run through me.

The Swamp King smiles wickedly, like I'm an insect he wants to crush, and I know in my soul he has every intention to do so. Amazingly, the man transforms into something new.

Standing from the wheelchair, he straightens like he was never infirmed but instead as normal as anyone. The goon pouring the liquor steps to the side and, from the darkness, finds a guitar—a BC Rich, I believe, by the style of it. Its starburst design and gloss bring a fine shine; it sparkles in the glow of the torches. In his hands, I figure the King doesn't have enough strength to hold the thing, much less play it.

"You ready, Remi?" the King says.

Breathing deep, I shore up my resolve enough to keep my nerves together. I need all I can to get this song out, but I feel I'm as ready as ever. It seems my whole life is made for this moment. I run a riff down Betty's neck, stretching and pulling the strings like making love to them, because in a nutshell, that's what's happening. Stopping at the bottom of the neck, I immediately run back up to the top and stop.

"Anytime," I say. Nervously, I wait to see what he'll do.

The sky rumbles above, uneasily, like the heavens are parting and the angels are watching in anticipation. Night covers everything, and no moon shines as dark clouds gather above.

An uneasy silence falls over the entire swamp as all eyes are on the King. From above, a long bolt of lightning hits the Swamp King. I wince, then adjust my eyes, watching the goons run for cover. The King shakes and pops, sizzling like bacon in a pan, until smoke rolls from his head and his body, causing him to convulse, flopping around like a fish. He falls onto the ground, lying there like a lump, the guitar to the side burning and looking as useless as the King himself.

Puzzling over this turn of events, I step forward to get a closer look at the man. Snitch and Carmichael are close to the edge of the swamp, ready to make a quick retreat I figure, but then I think about the treasure. They won't leave until they get their fair share.

My eyes widen when the King moves. His body jumps a couple times and then he stands, fully erect, the man useless no more. Char marks dot his face, making him look more intimidating than before. Hair stands on his head, wiry and unkempt, like Don King on his worst day.

Then the strangest thing happens. The guitar stands, spins on its bottom, then shoots toward the King like it's thrown from a sling, landing in the arms of its owner.

Charoon groans from the edge of the swamp as he lowers into the brackish water.

The King pops his neck, the crack reverberating through the sky above. His mouth produces a half smile, one side his lips, the other exposed bone. His fingers find the neck of the guitar, and with a quick move, he runs down it and back up so fast I barely register the movement.

Not one to let an opportunity go, I work Betty to keep up with the fury the King is producing. He drops a riff, and I match it, the fire of his music falling into mine, making for a melee of stretches and hammer on's and off, a false harmonic, and then I lay into the smaller frets, closer to the pickups.

There's where I do my best work. I give Betty a pet close to the top of the neck, running up and down the scales, then bring it high to where she screams, showing off her abilities. With each run, Betty says she ain't going down, she's going to fight whatever devils come from the night. Funny she says so, because as if to punctuate the point, the swamp starts moving.

First, things move from above, bats and the like, then crawling things, snakes and gators, come onto the grassy area around the camp. They pay no attention to us but scurry along, trying to find a place to hide.

Next, I find out what they're running from. Like Moses parted the Red Sea, the swamp separates, and creatures rise from the depths, moaning in a fashion I have never heard. Gravelly voices work into full-on screams. The night covers them, but as they come closer, I can see them clearly.

They're nasty things, with slimy moss hanging like spider webs covering the exposed bone between the ragged flesh. They're human-like in the sense they stand on two legs, but their arms are more like leeches, with tiny mouths opening and closing like they're breathing. Their heads are like gators, with long snouts and jagged teeth snapping the air. Sockets where eyes should be, they stare back at me, but I can't tell if they're sizing me up for a meal or blind to everything around them.

I choke back the fear and keep playing, running up and down the neck of the guitar with new ferocity, until they stop in front of me like they're in a trance.

The King plays too, but they pay him no attention, maybe because he brought them to the surface in the first place to distract me. It doesn't work because instead of being scared, I have new determination to play harder, running a new riff, one I've been working on for a while. The monsters don't seem impressed, but at least they're satiated, or so I think.

Snitch and Carmichael are close by, and the way I'm playing, I nearly forget about them. The two are backing slowly away when they notice the gator-like things moving in their direction, but they don't get far before the swamp things are upon them.

Blood curdling cries roll from Snitch as one sinks its teeth into his back. I try to look away, but it's hard to do. A hunk of flesh comes loose on his back, and he cries louder.

Deep down I know, I have an understanding you might say, if I quit playing, they'll turn on me too. So I don't stop even though those fools are getting what they deserve. You don't mess with a bocor like the Swamp King without paying for it in the end. I figure mine is coming too, eventually.

Another pins Carmichael to the ground with its leech-tentacle appendages, and my stomach turns when I hear the snap of bone from Carmichael's arm being twisted off. Then, as if things couldn't get worse, the creature puts the body part in its slimy mouth and starts chewing.

Even though the carnage is only a few feet away, I

keep playing, moving up and down the neck so fast I figure Betty will burst into flames. The King looks at me, the disdain in his eyes pure frustration, like he found a much more worthy opponent than he even thought.

The cries become weaker from Snitch and Carmichael until they're silent. The gator men continue their feast, the sound of bone crunching and slurping of blood and whatever innards they can eat filling my ears, producing a wave of nausea. I push it away and play another blistering riff, and the King counters, until we come to an intersection. The heat of the humid night produces sweat on my hands and forehead, making it hard to stay in the moment with the worry of missing a chord or note, but I keep going.

Waiting for the King to make the next move, I try to calm my breath. He stares at me with eyes intense but focused, like a lion on the Serengeti sizing up its next meal, with no vacancy, only raw determination.

Rolling his eyes and tilting his head back, the Swamp King's hands move on the guitar. His body thrusts against it, bucking forward with his hips, grinding in a ceremony of ecstasy, like he and his instrument are one in the same, and next, I see why. The guitar melts into him. I have never seen anything like it. The wooden thing becomes flexible, like rubber, then turns to liquid, melting into the King until he is no longer a man but the guitar itself.

In front of me, the man-instrument plays, and with no one picking or hammering, it seems to be playing effortlessly, melding into tunes of a sort I have never heard before, somewhere between melodic and technical, stretching and bending like an athlete trying to get the last bit of energy from their body. All manner of creeping things come out, crawling toward where the

King plays. It's like he's the Pied Piper taking the rats to the sea.

The game has intensified, as I know I can do no such thing. The only magic I possess is in my hands and the experience I've gained over years of playing. I play harder, matching note for note with the King, but I'm not playing hard enough to best him. If I keep this up, I'll tire long before him and this will be all for naught. The legend of Remi Martin will end out here in the middle of a swampy bayou.

Betty answers my doubts in kind, though. She won't give up on me, and I feel this deep in my very soul. A spell comes over me, and my tunes cause a ripple in the air. The night breaks apart, and I see figures emerging from the ground. Hands break through the earth, and I think this may be more monsters coming to help the ones that dispatched Snitch and Carmichael. But as they reveal themselves, I see I have nothing to fear.

Two men emerge from the dirt, then rise and stand in front of me as pieces of mud fall to their feet. My daddy and granddaddy notice me and smile. They say nothing but instead point to my guitar. Crackling energy like static in the air filters around me, coming from the men. I instantly feel energized again. Losing control of my fingers and hands, I move them along Betty's neck, up and down, hammering and pulling, hitting chords in the right spots, muting and stopping when need be. It's the magic I possessed all along—the ancestral heritage of a music man, given to me by my daddy and his before him.

Then, when I think it can get no better, my daddy and grandaddy sing. Melodies fill the air to accompany my playing. The Swamp King's playing no longer takes precedence but instead finds its way into the background, no longer of prominence, only a secondary tune on the B-side of the record.

I don't stop, and as my music intensifies, the heavens above open, with a bolt of lightning shooting through the air and raining down on the earth in various spots. It surprises everyone, even the monsters as they look away from their meal. Charoon lets out a loud whine, like a hound dog crying in distress. Insects stop chirping. All is silent for a moment except the low rumble of thunder. The King stops playing, then tries to pick up again but only produces a scratching sound.

Large bolts of electrical fire fall upon me, but this only heightens my ability to play as I absorb them into my hands. I have no control, taken over by the moment. Any abandon left in me falls away, and my fingers become their own entity like each one is a guitar player all by itself.

Betty and the spirituals my ancestors are singing produce a power even the Swamp King can't control. The electrical surge pumping through me branches to the King, and when the energy hits him, he transforms back to his original form, falling in a lump on the ground.

His wheelchair is gone, along with the goons helping him. He's a sniveling shell of a man who has no power left. The King rises onto his forearms, and with his last remaining strength, he murmurs an incantation of something. I can barely hear it over the cacophony of beautiful music filling the air around the swamp like angels in a choir.

Snakes and spiders crawl from the ground, making their way toward me. They don't get far as they're intercepted by my daddy. He steps on them, and each one pops with a blood sack explosion that pours across the ground to where the King lays.

The Swamp King screams as the blood covers him, creeping up his body like the snakes creep across the ground. The crimson liquid coats his body, filling his mouth and making him gag. He sputters as the music from me and my people heightens to a crescendo.

The gator men scream with ear-piercing protests, but the music drowns them out too, until they explode on the spot. The Swamp King is no match for the power I've brought, and he finally collapses, sinking into the blood-covered ground, reaching and clawing for purchase.

I stop playing, and the singing lightens to a murmur. The only thing I hear is the last gurgling complaints of the King as they fade into the night.

My daddy and grandaddy turn to me and smile as they sink into the ground, the dirt piling over them until they vanish like they were never there at all. I'm left alone, with Betty by my side.

Kneeling by the guitar case, I release the shoulder strap holding her to me and place her gently into her nest once more. "Thanks, girl, you saved my life again."

A noise startles me to attention, a groan from close to the edge of the swamp. A large shadow I recognize looms there in the dark, holding something.

Charoon drops to one knee and hands me a box made of bones. It's off white and dirty, like it's very old. He sets it in front of me, and I notice latches on the front. Undoing them, I open the lid to the box, and light glitters the color of gold in my eyes. It's the Swamp King's treasure.

"Thank you, Charoon."

The large man-beast nods to me and makes a sound less like a groan and more like a cooing.

Nodding to the boat, I ask, "Think I can get a ride back

to the car?"

In minutes, I'm floating along, treasure in hand, and lying back, not as nervous as I was when I came here. I suppose I am the best around, but if I'm honest, there probably are a few better. I guess I won't know until another one comes along to challenge me. I'll tell them to get in line, because Betty might have something to say about it.

WAMPUS

TIMOTHY KING

"**B**illy, slow down!"

Sandy pushed through the bushes, shielding her face from the menacing sticks that scratched at her skin. One of her feet sank into the mud. Her face twisted up in anger as murky water filled her shoes. "Billy!"

Billy whipped around. "Come on!" he called back to her. "We're gonna miss the party."

She shook her head. "I want to go back." She scanned the swampy terrain. They were deep into the Everglades, or at least deeper than she had ever been. She kicked herself for letting Billy talk her into risking their lives for a dumb high school party.

"Dad's going to kill us if he finds out!"

He ignored her and pushed through another thicket of trees. "It's only a little further!"

"Seriously! What about the Wampus Cat?"

Billy came to an abrupt halt and whirled around with an incredulous expression on his face. "You don't ..."

He stared back at his sister for a moment before a grin stretched across his face. "You don't actually believe in the Wampus Cat, do you?"

Sandy looked down. "No, but Dad said ..."

He cut her off by holding a finger out to silence her.

The rhythmic beat of a Luke Bryan song rolled through the air, interrupting their awkward exchange. His smile grew even wider.

Sandy rolled her eyes. She pictured a bunch of horny, half-drunk teenagers grinding on each other around a keg. The whole thing would have been ripped right out of a movie.

The music grew louder as they approached.

She put her head down and trudged through the mud and bushes.

Billy stopped a few feet ahead of her, allowing her an opportunity to catch up. "You gotta keep up," he muttered.

The song changed to something else that pretended to be country but was obviously an excuse to make girls in Daisy Dukes shake their asses.

"Really?" she asked. "You want to hang out with people who listen to this shit?"

Billy jerked his head in her direction. "Kelly invited me to this party," he said with a shit-eating grin. "I'd jam out to opera music if that's what she was into."

The two pushed on toward the sound of music. It grew louder with each step, acting as a siren's song drawing them in. The acrid smell of smoke grew stronger with their approach as well. Through the trees, they could see the warm glow of a massive bonfire. It seemed to struggle for dominance against the dying light of the evening.

"We made it," Billy said, his voice giddy with

excitement. He pushed forward, heading for the clearing.

A stick cracked behind them.

Sandy spun around and scanned the forest for any sign of disturbance. The uneasy sensation of being watched fell over her, causing her skin to break out in goosebumps.

"Billy, did you ..." She let her words drift off as Billy left the cover of the forest and entered the clearing. She stole a look back in the woods before following her brother into the mass of dancing teenagers.

Jacked-up trucks with their doors open and tailgates down ringed the clearing. Girls Sandy recognized from high school but had never spoken to danced provocatively in the beds of those trucks, shaking their asses in time with the beat of the music. Jocks and rednecks intermingled, drinking beer from red Solo cups and laughing obnoxiously.

She shook her head. "This town is a walking cliche," she muttered to herself, following Billy into the party.

The sun was setting behind the trees, backlighting the scene with a pink sky.

Sandy pushed into the crowd after her brother but lost him almost immediately. He either found Kelly or his football buddies. Either way, she was on her own.

She continued through the throng of people, trying to avoid the sweaty bodies. A large guy in a red shirt bumped into her, causing her to lose her balance and stumble into a mud puddle. Her Converse sank to her ankle, flooding the inside of the shoe with a cold, murky soup. She yanked her foot out of the mud with a squelch and turned to face the guy who bumped into her.

"Fuck, dude, I'm so sorry," he said.

Sandy didn't recognize him. She wasn't popular by any

stretch of the imagination, but they went to a very small school, and there was no way she wouldn't have noticed the beautiful specimen of a man standing before her.

"Can I get you a drink?" His eyes drifted down to her mud-caked shoes. "Or I might have a towel in my truck?"

Everything inside her wanted to be her normal, snarky self, but something in his eyes convinced her he was being genuine. She forced on a smile and nodded. "A beer would be awesome."

The handsome boy smiled, revealing perfectly straight, white teeth. Between that and his blond hair, the guy looked like he had been built in a lab.

He reached out and took her hand, sending a wave of excitement rolling through her body. "Come on," he beckoned.

She allowed him to guide her through the crowd until they reached a beer keg sitting on ice.

The boy grabbed a Solo cup from a pack on the ground, filled it with beer, then passed it to her.

Sandy tilted the cup slightly in thanks and took a sip. She had never been one to enjoy beer, but it was better than being sober at a high school party in the middle of a swamp.

"My name's Cannon, by the way," the handsome boy said, stretching out a hand.

Sandy shook it and smiled. "Thanks for the beer, Cannon." She nodded at him playfully. "I'm Sandy."

"Beautiful name for a beautiful girl," he said with a wink.

Sandy rolled her eyes. "That was awful!" she exclaimed with a laugh.

He chuckled and shook his head. "I'm sorry! I'm terrible at this. First I bump into you and ruin your shoe, and now I hit you with a cheesy pickup line."

She turned away from Cannon and looked back over her shoulder with a devilish smile. "Well, it's working," she said, before walking away from the party and toward the woods.

Cannon stood there dumbfounded for a moment. He looked back and forth from the party to Sandy several times before turning and jogging after her.

Sandy retreated farther into the woods, her heart slamming against her chest. She had never done anything like that before; hell, she had only ever kissed one boy. But something about the way Cannon looked at her made her want to take a risk.

"So, uh, what grade are you in?" Cannon called out as he struggled to catch up with her.

She looked back over her shoulder and smiled before turning around and leaning against a tree. "I'm a junior," she said.

He nodded as he approached. "I'll be a senior this year, just transferred in from out of state." He closed the distance between them and rested one hand against the tree she was leaning on.

She looked up at him and bit her lip.

A massive smile spread across his face. "Can I, uh," he stuttered, "can I kiss you?"

She smiled and nodded her head.

He leaned in for a kiss.

Just as their lips were about to touch, a rustling noise to their right pulled her attention away. She jerked her head, causing Cannon's lips to brush against her cheek.

He reeled back. "I'm sorry," he muttered. "We don't have ..."

Sandy shot a finger to his lips to silence him. "Did you hear that?"

He shook his head. "It's probably a trash panda."

She gave him a curious look. "A trash panda?"

Throwing his head back in an exaggerated laugh, he said, "Yeah, that's what my family calls raccoons."

Sandy giggled and put her hand on Cannon's chest. "I'm sorry. I always get freaked out when I come out to the swamps."

"You're safe with me," he whispered, leaning in to complete the kiss they had started.

Their lips brushed against each others. Heat flushed through Sandy's face. She couldn't believe she was kissing a boy she just met. Everyone always told her to live a little, so that was what she would do.

She placed her hand on Cannon's cheek, ready to keep the kiss going all night, when a low rumble emanated from somewhere behind him. Against her wishes, she tore her lips away from his and leaned to see around his large frame.

"Seriously, you didn't hear that?" she whispered.

He sighed. "It's probably a stray cat or something, but if it makes you feel better, I'll go check it out." He took a few small steps away from her. "Don't go anywhere." He winked at her, then spun around and marched into the darkness.

Sandy dragged the toe of her ruined shoe through a patch of dirt, fidgeting impatiently as she waited for him to return. After what felt like a couple minutes, she took a few hesitant steps in the direction he went.

"Cannon?" She was met by the buzzing of bugs and the rustling of leaves in the wind. "Cannon? Seriously, I'm getting a little creeped out."

She stumbled forward in the nearly complete darkness, the distant glow of the bonfire her only source of light. Pushing through a thick patch of bushes, her foot sank into something warm and wet. Her hands flew to her pocket, fumbling to drag her phone out and turn on the flashlight. The light burst to life, blinding her for the briefest of moments before the scene in front of her formed into a coherent image.

Cannon lay on his back, his lifeless eyes staring up into hers. Blood bubbled up through massive gashes in his throat before spilling over the edges and racing down the sides of his neck to coagulate on the muddy ground.

Sandy's hands flew to her mouth. It took several seconds before she could catch her breath enough to manage a scream. Her cry rang out through the trees to compete with the deafening sound of the party. She screamed again and again, her brain completely shutting down and unable to process the scene before her.

After her third scream, the sound of the music died down, replaced with the frantic cries of teenage boys entering the woods. She heard them marching toward her and calling out to anyone in the woods, but she couldn't bring herself to answer.

Squeezing her eyes shut, she focused on taking a deep breath and holding it for ten seconds, a trick her father taught her to deal with her fears.

When she opened her eyes again, she didn't see Cannon's corpse. Instead, she fixated on a pair of bright, yellow eyes staring back at her from beneath a large bush. The primal, animalistic part of her brain reacted before she could formulate a coherent thought. She turned and sprinted as fast as she could in the direction of the party, using the voices of the other teenagers as her beacon in the darkness.

She pushed through some bushes before her foot slipped in a pile of dead vegetation, sending her sprawling forward on all fours, landing between two of the larger football players from her high school.

"Holy shit, Sandy! Are you ok?"

Sandy's face flushed, first at the realization that this popular boy knew her name, then immediately at the realization that she needed their help.

"Cannon!" she screamed, pointing the way she had come.

"What about him?" the other boy asked.

"Was he being a fucking creep?" the first boy asked. He smacked the other boy on the shoulder. "Told you we couldn't trust that pretty boy."

Sandy shook her head, fighting to catch her breath. "No!" She scrambled back to her feet. "He's dead!"

The two boys looked from Sandy to each other before bursting out laughing. "Ok, Sandy." One of the boys mocked her. "That's a good one."

The other boy barked out a laugh and pushed past Sandy, walking toward the area she had just come from. "Alright, Cannon! Quit fucking around!" The large football player pushed a tree limb out of his way and squinted into the darkness. "What the ..." His words trailed off, only to be replaced with a blood-curdling scream.

Something massive launched itself through the air, pouncing on the boy and sending him plummeting to the ground. The jet-black skin of an enormous animal rippled with muscles as Sandy's flashlight beam danced across it. The creature threw its head back and released an ear-piercing shriek before its mouth descended onto the boy's face.

The crunching of bones and the squelching of blood filled the air, replacing the boy's choked cries for help.

"Brian!" the other boy yelled. In one athletic movement, he sprinted forward, stopped to grab a large stick off the ground, and swung it at the beast.

The beast bounced away, landing firmly on all four of its massive paws before exploding forward once again and raking its claws across the boy's stomach.

Sandy watched in horror as the boy slowly turned around, his entrails uncoiling through his eviscerated abdomen like a coil of purple ropes. She stumbled backward a few steps, fear once again shutting down her brain.

The creature stalked around the boy until it was behind him. She could do nothing but watch as it leaped onto his back and buried its fangs deep into the back of his neck.

Not wanting to see any more of the carnage, she spun on her heels and sprinted through the trees and into the clearing.

The entire party was stopped, and a hundred pairs of eyes rested solely on her.

Billy slowly stepped forward, pushing through the crowd. "Sandy?" He asked it at first, waiting for his brain to catch up with the terrified appearance of his sister. "Shit," he muttered. Rushing forward, he grabbed her shoulders. "What happened?"

She pointed back at the woods. "W-w-wampus," she stuttered.

"What?"

She shook her finger angrily at the trees behind her. "The fucking Wampus Cat!!!"

Billy looked from his sister to the trees, then rolled his eyes. "Are you fucking kidding me with this shit?" he hissed in her ear.

She shook her head, tears welling up in her eyes. "Seriously, Billy, it's fucking real!"

Billy grabbed her by the arm and dragged her toward one of the pickup trucks and away from the prying eyes of the partygoers. "Don't do this," he whispered. "It's my senior year, and I think I have a real shot with Kelly."

Sandy smacked Billy's hand away from her. "This isn't a fucking joke, Billy!"

"Billy? Is everything ok?" a soft feminine voice asked.

The siblings broke their standoff and turned their attention to a young blonde walking toward them.

Billy shook his head. "Yeah, we're good. My sister just freaked herself out by wandering off into the swamp."

Kelly flashed Sandy a warm smile. "That's OK, I've done that before too," she said in her most reassuring tone. She opened her mouth to say something else, but a low growl from the nearby trees cut her off.

A scream broke through the air. The trio whipped around to see another boy on the ground. Blood poured from an open wound on his neck. He tried to stifle the bleeding with his hands, but it seeped through the cracks of his fingers, coating the front of his chest.

As if a dam had broken, the sea of people scrambled in every direction. Screaming teenagers piled into trucks, disappeared into the surrounding trees, and trampled over one another.

Sandy watched in horror as the large, black cat-like thing she witnessed killing the other boys rampaged through the crowd, brutally mauling one teenager after another.

She watched it pounce on a girl from her third-period math class before dragging its enormous claws along the girl's back, shredding her with no apparent effort.

"We gotta go!" Billy's voice cut through the chaos. His hand gripped Sandy's arm firmly. "Sandy! Let's fucking go!"

Sandy spun around and followed Billy and Kelly into the woods. They sprinted through the darkness, away from the sounds of the carnage behind them. They ran until Sandy's legs and chest burned. She wanted to stop but wasn't sure how far they had gone or how far was far enough.

To her relief, Kelly broke first.

"I have to stop," she said in an exasperated voice. "I can't keep running."

Billy stopped running and turned to face the girls. "What was that thing?"

Sandy sucked in a labored breath before answering. "It's the Wampus Cat! I was in the woods with Cannon and it killed him."

"Oh my god," Kelly whispered. "What do we do?"

Billy shook his head. "I'm calling Dad."

Sandy grabbed his arm as he raised his cell phone to his ear. "He doesn't know we snuck out," she protested. "We'll be grounded forever."

"It's better than being dead!" He pressed the dial button on the phone and put it on speaker.

After three rings, their father answered the phone, sounding groggy. "Billy?" he asked.

"Yeah, Dad. We need your help."

"What's going on?" Their dad's voice instantly lost any semblance of drowsiness.

"We're at a party in the swamp." Billy looked at Sandy, trying to figure out how to describe what just happened.

"It was the Wampus Cat, Daddy," Sandy blurted out before Billy could decide what to say next.

The line went silent for a few seconds as the trio waited for a response. "Ok." Their father's voice was flat and emotionless. "You two listen to me, and listen good."

The siblings looked at each other, their fear mirrored in each other's eyes.

"The Wampus Cat will not stop hunting you until you

are out of the swamp. It never leaves the bayou." He paused again and seemed to be contemplating what to say next. "Do you know where you are?"

Sandy shook her head, but Billy nodded.

"Yeah, Dad. We came in off Route 19 and parked at the dead end off Mile Marker 50. We walked south for about fifteen minutes until we hit a clearing."

Their father grunted into the phone. "Ok, the fastest way out of the swamp is exactly the way you came in."

"It killed some people," Sandy whispered.

Their father sighed. "And it will kill more before the night's over. You run for the car and do not stop. I'm calling the sheriff and sending him to meet you at the car. I'll be there as soon as I can. And kids?"

"Yeah?" they answered simultaneously.

"I love you both very much." An uncomfortable silence hung in the air for a few moments before their father broke again. "Now run," he commanded, and ended the call.

Billy turned the flashlight on his phone back on and looked around. "I think we need to go this way," he said in a shaky voice.

"Are you sure?" Kelly asked.

"No," he admitted, "but it's my best guess."

"Anything's better than standing here waiting for it to find us," Sandy hissed. Without waiting for a response, she turned and pushed through the thick brush.

The trio marched through the swamp as quickly as they could. Their shoes sank in thick mud, creating loud, suction-cup-like sounds as they struggled along slowly. In the distance, the sounds of screaming teenagers echoed through the trees, the screams becoming less and less frequent as the minutes ticked by.

Sandy looked down at her mosquito-bitten legs. Pain

radiated up from her sore feet. She knew better than to wear Converse on her trip through the Everglades, but at the time, looking cool seemed more important.

Sandy was so lost in thoughts of Cannon and what could have been that she didn't realize the others had stopped in front of her. She smacked into the back of Kelly, nearly sending her face-first into the mud.

"Shhh," Billy hissed. He made a downward motion with his hand and crouched.

The girls followed his lead.

The crack of a branch pulled their attention to the right. A teenage boy's head popped up from the bushes as he crept forward.

Billy squinted his eyes against the darkness, trying to figure out who it was. A smile stretched across his face. He leaped to his feet and waved a hand.

"Mikey!"

The boy turned and locked eyes with Billy. His eyes stretched wide, and he shook his head before dropping back into the bushes.

"What the fuck is his problem?" Billy whispered.

A growl rose up from behind them. Slowly, the trio turned to see yellow eyes staring down at them from a tree. They stood frozen in that moment, each unsure what to do, until Billy finally spoke. "Run!"

He turned and sprinted in the direction they had been traveling.

Sandy was the next to react, pushing past Kelly and chasing after her brother.

Kelly took a few hesitant steps backward before turning and chasing after the others.

They sprinted through the darkness, slipping in the mud, tripping over debris on the ground. The hiss of the Wampus Cat was a constant reminder that they were mere seconds from death. The beast leaped from tree to tree, covering the distance between the teenagers and itself in seconds.

Sandy glanced up in horror as the monstrosity landed in a tree to her right. It touched down briefly, launching itself into the air almost as soon as its enormous paws hit the branch.

"Billy! Duck!" she screamed.

Billy reacted quickly and crumpled to the ground.

The Wampus Cat flew over his head, its claws missing his neck by a hair, and disappeared into a thicket of bushes.

Billy looked up and then back to Sandy as she sprinted toward him. His eyes were stretched wide in fear. She grabbed him by his shirt collar as she rushed past him, yanking him to his feet. He slipped in mud before finding his footing and chasing after his sister.

The smack of Kelly's feet echoed behind them.

A garish light broke through the trees ahead of them, accompanied by the squeal of brakes bringing a car to an abrupt halt.

Relief flooded Sandy's body. They were almost out of the swamp. She leaned forward, pumping her arms harder.

Behind her, the Wampus Cat roared. The heavy thud of its feet rose up to challenge their own footfalls and panting for dominance of the otherwise-silent forest.

Sandy covered her face and exploded through the bushes. A large stretch of open grass stretched out in front of her before ending in a paved parking lot. Her eyes flicked up to her father's worried face.

He beckoned her forward, screaming something about running.

Her heart beat furiously in her chest. She looked back

to see Billy explode through the trees. He collapsed to the ground at her side, and operating purely on instinct, she squatted down and grabbed him under the arm. "Let's go!"

"Don't leave me!" Kelly's voice rang out from within the trees.

Sandy looked back in time to see Kelly emerge through the trees before falling to her stomach. Massive gashes crisscrossed her back. Ruined muscle and tissue pushed through the cuts in her tattered shirt. She reached a hand toward Sandy, desperation in her eyes. "Please," she whimpered.

Sandy took a step toward her but stopped. Her veins flooded with ice as two yellow eyes shone in the darkness just behind Kelly. The Wampus Cat stepped forward, its body seeming to absorb the light from her father's car, making the area around the beast seem unnaturally dark. It slowly extended one of its paws as if daring Sandy to stop it. The beast's claws sank into Kelly's calf, causing rivers of blood to spew forth like a tidal wave.

Kelly cried out in pain. "Please!" she begged one final time.

With a loud screech, the monster yanked her backward. She slid across the ground before disappearing back into the darkness of the bayou. Her choked cries faded into the night.

"Kids! Let's go!"

Sandy felt a firm hand on her shoulder pulling her toward the car.

"Come on, Sandy! We've got to get out of here!"

Sandy allowed her brother to drag her to the car. She collapsed into the back seat, the image of Kelly's face replaying in her mind's eye.

Her father threw the car in reverse and backed out of the parking lot. They drove in silence as police cruisers with flashing blue and red lights rushed past them, heading toward the swamps.

"I can't believe it's real," Billy muttered.

Their father looked from the road to Billy and back again. "I tried to warn you kids." He turned in his seat to look back at Sandy. "Never go into the bayou. The Wampus Cat will get you."

The Bayou Demands Its Toll

William F. Gray

"You all heard the phrase '... is an unforgiving place?'" Anyone can plug pretty much anything in front of those four words and get an ominous, if not downright frightening, saying to scare the little kids. Hell, some adults even.

"The bayou is worse. It's got a long memory, and it doesn't forget. It swallows things whole, but they don't disappear. Not completely. They may be gone to you and me, but they'll always be part of the swamp, which seems as much a living organism itself as it is an entire ecosystem filled with life of different kind. People bring things here to be forgotten and only seem to succeed.

"The police may never discover that gun, your wife might never learn about the secrets you keep, but the bayou knows. It doesn't speak, but that doesn't mean it doesn't judge. Who's to say those things aren't waiting for you on the other side? That when you cross over, you won't find that briefcase covered in mud and algae, stinking of decay, or the man you murdered holding that gun, bayou water still dripping from the tip of its barrel? That ..."

"Pete, shut the fuck UP!" Grayson finally exclaims over the steady drone of the engine, the vein on his thick, muscular neck pulsing. "I can't fucking think!"

The boat—an old, mold-covered skimmer—rocks as Pete shifts in his seat near the rear. I notice he's careful to keep his feet to the side and away from the shape at the bottom of the boat.

The Louisiana night is dark out in the bayou. It's impossible to shake the feeling of the supernatural, and Pete's campfire spiel has only made it worse.

Grayson cuts the boat to the left, narrowly missing a tree that's nearly submerged in the opaque, still water.

"Cut it back, Gray," I tell him. "The last thing we need is to get stranded out here with ..."

"I know what I'm doing, Everett. Just shut your mouth, man."

Tension is running high. Tempers are flaring. A quick glance back at Pete tells me he's about ready to ask Grayson to cash the check he's writing. I imagine a fist fight in this small skimmer, can see one or both of them going overboard. And then it's just me and *him*.

Grayson has tied off both ends of the tarp wrapped around the shape, and I can clearly see the outline of a head where the ropes are taut around its neck. *His* neck.

What the hell have we gotten ourselves into?

I try to remember how it all played out, try to remember if we saw the motion-detecting light kick or heard the livestock first. *Chicken or the egg?* It doesn't matter, because they both led to the fucking dead guy at the bottom of the boat.

"How much further do we have to go?" Pete whines.

"As far as we can take it," Grayson answers.

The man was in the backyard, the wire doors to the chicken coops wide open. I was the first one out despite it being Grayson's house. We were still in our grease-stained overalls, simple navy because the local auto shop didn't splurge for logos.

Hell, we still *are* in them. Now they're filthy in a different way. Pete's pants legs are soaked with swamp water from where he pushed us from shore, and I can see just how much darker the cuffs are of Grayson's. Blood turns the fabric there almost black in the dark night.

We have to do this, I think. Repeat it. This is all Grayson's idea, and for good reason. The three of us might not seem like we have a lot to lose, but there's something much more valuable than money.

Freedom.

I did four years for stealing guns from my stepfather. I was going to sell them for dope money, but instead, I got caught four miles from the house and was sent upstate.

Pete wrote enough bad checks with old ladies names on them to earn himself a couple felonies and six months in jail after a plea deal.

And Grayson scarred his knuckles from accidentally beating a man to death in a drunken rage. His family had money, and they used it to help sweep it under the rug as best as they could. He still ended up serving three years in the same penitentiary I found myself in, but once his time was up, it wasn't his family waiting at the gate for him when he came strutting out in clothes that no longer fit.

He was dead to them, so he had me.

In short, all three of us are convicted felons. None of us should have guns. And even though it's only one of us who does carry, all three of us are in it together the moment things escalate.

"What the hell was I supposed to do?" Grayson says as if reading my mind. "That dude was *crazy*. He was trespassing. You saw what he did."

I absolutely did.

I'll never forget how his mangled, rotting teeth sank into the neck of the chicken, how his gums bled almost as bad as the chicken when he ripped its head off with one fell swoop of his arm, his loose teeth barely holding on to the poor creature's head.

"Probably PCP," Pete says, rejoining the competition. "Some of the guys in jail said they'd seen those tweakers do some crazy shit."

"Exactly. And he was coming for us next. It was self-defense."

I know this is the truth.

Grayson didn't fire the first shot until the guy dropped the chicken and came at us, but this doesn't make him feel any better about it. Because that argument is null and void should we be discovered. I imagine exactly what he would try to tell the police.

It was self-defense, officer. It was him or us, so after it was done, we wrapped the guy up in a tarp, stole a skimmer from the edge of the swamp, and motored out here to get rid of the body. Just drop him in the water and let him sink and forget the whole thing because, you know, we're innocent.

I stifle a laugh. Everything about this is so fucked.

The steady chug of the motor changes, as if the karmic forces of the universe have finally taken notice of us. Maybe it's my fault, but then again, we wouldn't be in this mess without Grayson, so it's at least a shared responsibility.

It starts as a choppy sputtering accompanied by the stench of burned oil. Black smoke emanates from the ventilation on either side, and I can hear Pete curse as he hits the damned thing. My eyes are on Grayson, who turns from the controls at the bow of the skimmer and stares at us.

"What the fuck happened?"

"We stole a piece of shit," Pete snaps back. He immediately kills the mounted engine and turns to face our friend.

The acrid stench of the ruined motor is too much for me to take. My head begins to pound from it, or maybe it's the stress of what it means. I cast a glance at the body wrapped in a polyester tarp at our feet.

My stomach turns when I see it move.

Just shifting, I tell myself, settling from the change in momentum, the sudden decrease of motion. Because there's no way that fucker is still alive with a bullet in his chest and another in his head.

"Well, we can't just *sit* here!" Grayson complains, his voice raising an octave. I've never heard him sound so afraid, not even when he was convinced the police were going to show up in the middle of our frantic efforts to get the man wrapped up, get him to the car, get him into this goddamned boat we stole from the dock—

"We gotta dump him here," Pete says. I imagine he's itching to pace back and forth, anything but stand directly over the body in the boat, but there's no room. "There's probably oars or something we can use to get back to shore."

"Nah, not far enough. Any Joe Shmoe could come by here doing god knows what and find him. We need to drop him deeper into the swamp, where no one is likely to ..."

My eyes widen as the body moves. The boat is growing still in the water, and what I just witnessed is not some transfer of energy. It's not momentum.

"*Guys,*" I interject, but I don't think they can hear me. They carry on, and I raise my voice. "*Guys!*"

Both of them turn toward me, their expressions near-identical masks of fear and frustration. I imagine the two of them yelling *what* in unison, but the corpse at the bottom of the boat sits up and screams before they can.

All three of us stumble backward at the same, trying to create distance between us and the impossible thing we're witnessing. My eyes are locked on its mouth, where I can see the shape of its lips as the raspy screech escapes its chest and rattles the night around us. It threatens to break reality, or at least our sanity.

In my peripheral vision, I see Pete's legs strike the edge of the boat.

Oh, FUCK.

It happens in my mind's eye a split second before it does in real life. Pete's face shifts from downright fear toward shock, but the terror is still there. His fall seems impossibly slow as gravity pulls him down and into the murky water at the rear of the boat.

The splash is deafening.

"Pete!" I yell, and I suddenly become aware of just how quiet the swamp has become. The familiar drone of insects is completely gone. All that's left are the corpse's screams.

Then that ceases. I watch as the tarp sucks inward around its lips. Expecting panicked breathing, I'm surprised as the man inside begins to *chew*. His teeth gnash at the polyester like a rat trying to chew through rope. Within seconds, the first black hole appears in the sea of blue.

I turn toward Grayson, and the dread I'm experiencing only deepens. He stands just outside of the small shelter surrounding the boat controls; the pistol in his hands shakes as he aims it at the horrific scene playing out before us.

There's a moment when I think he'll pull the trigger, but then I notice the look in his eyes.

It's only once my eyes are off of the corpse behind me that I realize it's doing more than chewing through its horrific prison.

It's *whispering*.

I can't make out what it's saying underneath the sounds of its working jaw and the tearing material of the tarp, but there are syllables there. Non-sensical, maybe, but there's something deliberate.

When Grayson removes one hand and rotates his wrist, I take a step back out of reflex. Then I realize I'm closer to the thing we came out here to be rid of, the thing that's *supposed to be dead.* The thing that's most assuredly *not* dead.

"Grayson ..." I say, my voice barely audible over the ripping and gnashing behind me.

"The bayou is hungry." His voice is dreamy, almost

ethereal, as he presses the pistol to his temple. *"Ravenous. It demands a toll.... It must be fed."*

The gunshot rings out, and I watch as everything that makes Grayson who he is flies out of the other side of his skull. Blood paints the night, splashes of it hitting the murky window of the control room beside Grayson, and the side of the boat a bit farther along, before chunks of brain matter and bone hit the water with a series of loud *plops.*

Cold suddenly seeps into me despite the humid night. Fingers, invisible but tangible, begin to worm their way through my clothes, through my *skin,* and search blindly.

The whispering picks up, the phrases spoken impossible to decipher, yet I understand. I turn toward the corpse, this impossible thing, and wish I knew more about it.

Is this thing always of the bayou, some creature that we don't understand, or did it creep into the flesh of this dead man we brought here to make disappear?

Maybe it doesn't matter.

I become aware of dark shapes emerging from the water, strangely humanoid in this horrible place. They're oily smudges in the night. Seeing them sends adrenaline-induced terror through my veins like electricity down the third rail.

Without thinking about it, I dive for the gun that's still in Grayson's hand. I pry it from his already cooling grip and raise it to fire, but an explosion of sound from the rear of the skimmer surprises me. Swinging the pistol around, I fire several shots into the bayou water.

"Stop, stop!" The voice is broken up by sputtering as the owner gasps for air. It's also familiar.

Pete.

"Shit, shit, *shit,*" I mutter, crawling toward my friend as he splashes in the murky water. The corpse is still sitting up, still whispering, its voice trying to work whatever magic it used to force Grayson to kill himself. There's not enough room for me to avoid it the way I would like, so I climb over its feet and reach the rear edge of the boat.

"Help me out here, man!" Pete yells. He's near the edge of the boat, but I barely register that.

I'm too focused on the shadowy figures that are mere feet from him. Closing in.

"Pete, look out!"

I watch as he turns in a semi-circle, but it's too late. He doesn't stand a chance.

They pounce on him, closing the distance before he can even scream. They're shapes without details as they swarm him like a herd of predators hunting a single prey. The water swallows up the tangle of dark bodies.

Pete learns the hard way that he was right about the unforgiving nature of the bayou.

Still whispering.

The voice behind me is unrelenting and picking up speed. Those invisible probing fingers find something they like, and I feel a sharp pain in the back of my head. It doubles me over the side of the boat, the agony so sudden and severe that I let go of the pistol and hear it splash into the water below. My right hand shoots out after it out of reflex, and I let out a bloodcurdling scream as something grabs my wrist.

No, no, no!

I can't die like this. After everything, all I want is a chance. I'm not even the one that killed the fucking guy, or thing, or whatever the fuck it is.

I pull myself to my feet, groaning as the pressure

increases, and I feel my shoulder pop out of place. My eyes fall on the motor to my left, and I remember that acrid, burning smell. There's very little chance it'll start, but I have nothing else within feet of me except for the whispering corpse.

The agony is almost unbearable as I use my free hand and grab the pull cord on the motor. *Please, God, help me out with this one.*

The motor roars to life with one swift yank. The boat leaps forward, and I experience another miracle: when the engine died, Grayson failed to kill the throttle. If he had, the boat never would have started. My surprise is short-lived as I'm reminded of the danger I'm in by a fresh wave of pain.

Looking down at the dark shape of the humanoid creature in the water, I plant both feet on the edge of the boat and drag it into the path of the propeller, which is sputtering again. Blood and flesh spray in an arc as the thing's face is shredded by the blades. They chip away at the bone of its face before getting stuck, and the grip of its hand slowly loses its strength.

The engine groans and dies again, this time with a black billow of smoke that makes the previous one look like it was nothing but a small cough.

The hand slowly slips away from my wrist into the water.

Behind me, the corpse suddenly ceases its whispering and collapses onto the deck of the boat, the hole it chewed yawning wide. The icy probing stops along with it, and the sounds of the bayou resume.

I collapse onto my ass, searching the dark around me for any signs of the figures lurking in the water. When I find I'm alone, I cry with relief.

Then I look over the edge of the boat and see the

horrific sight in the water.

The humanoid creature is gone, replaced with the floating corpse of my friend. His face is destroyed, the blades of the propeller that did the damage still embedded in the freshly revealed bone.

I let out a scream that only the bayou will be able to hear.

I can't help but imagine that it smiles in reply, satiated.

GOTTA FERTILIZE THE DEMON

TONY EVANS

The storm had just started to creep onto the horizon as Seth and Katie walked out of the Saint Star diner and got back into their SUV. It had been completely unexpected, and as far as either of them could tell, there hadn't even been a chance of rain in the forecast, let alone a whole fucking storm.

For the past two days, they had driven, starting in Minnesota, a brief stay in Louisville, then back on the road as they headed toward Charleston, South Carolina ... and the entire time, they had been graced with the most beautiful weather they could've asked for. Clear blue skies except for a few puffy cumulus clouds over Kentucky, bright sunshine, temps in the high 70s and low 80s, and not a goddamn worry in the world.

But none of that mattered at that moment, and neither did the last weather report they'd heard before leaving the interstate some fifteen miles back that called for the stalled high pressure system to continue bringing dry, near-perfect weather their way. None of that mattered, because regardless of what anyone had said, the sky had suddenly filled with thick, dark, hostile clouds—clouds that appeared angry, clouds that took on a strange red and purple hue as they blocked out the last vestiges of sunlight on the South Carolina horizon. It was obvious to anyone with a brain that a storm was imminent.

"Well," Katie said, swiping her phone's screen as she tried to get the weather app to load. "What do you think we should do? Stop, or hope we can outrun it?"

Seth stared up at the sky like a disappointed child that didn't get their way. He was trying to decide what was best or, more accurately, what was safest. It wasn't like they had a ton of options, being more than 1200 miles from home. They could either get back on the interstate and chance getting caught in whatever was coming, or they could pull over and get a room for the night and make the last leg of the trip in the morning, hopefully once everything cleared.

Charleston was only a couple hours away at that point, plus or minus, and a couple hours was nothing compared to all the driving they had already done. But Seth was a realist when it came to his limits. He wasn't twenty years old anymore, and though he certainly wasn't what he would consider *old*, though his back may have told a different story, his vision had gotten worse over the years. If he was being honest with himself, it didn't take much rain at all, especially at night, to give him trouble seeing. Throw in headlights glaring off the windshield and a wet pavement surface, and he really struggled.

Seth sighed, knowing what was probably best, but also

knowing that they were *so close* to their destination. "I don't know. What's the radar look like?"

Katie swiped again, but the only thing visible was an annoying circle rotating in the center of the screen. "I'd love to tell you, but it won't load." She swiped the app again, the frustration obvious in the amount of force she applied. She realized that pushing and dragging on the screen with more force wouldn't make any difference in the app's ability to load, but it made her feel better in the moment.

"Think it's the storm causing issues maybe?" Seth sat straight up, baring his teeth. "Or ... I mean, we are out in the middle of nowhere. Maybe you don't have service."

"No, I had it when we got off the interstate. I definitely ... " She trailed off as her focus shifted to the top right of the screen. "*Don't* have service. Well, *fuck* me," she grumbled. "Great."

Seth shook his head and chuckled. "Seems about right," he said as he pulled his phone out to check too. They had the same carrier, so he knew his phone wouldn't magically have bars, but he had to see for himself nonetheless. "Oh, look at that. Fucking SOS. That's helpful." He looked to Katie, then back to the sky. The reds and purples swirled together, and small hints of dark green had started to mix in. He sighed deeply and laughed. "I guess I'll at least be able to call for help if it comes to that."

In the distance, the sky brightened as the first strike of lightning streaked across the sky.

Seth knew the right thing to do, knew what was best. They both did. There really wasn't any doubt in their minds. Whatever was coming, it didn't look like it would blow over quickly, and it *definitely* looked like it was going to be rough. As much as either of them hated to say it, and as much as Seth, specifically, just wanted to be at the beach when he woke up, the risk of getting stuck out there in it or, worse, the risk of getting into an accident just wasn't worth it.

"Doesn't look good, does it?" Katie said.

A light gust of wind came through, and a single large drop of rain hit the windshield, followed by another, then another. Somewhere far away, the low rumble of thunder echoed. The storm was getting closer.

"No, it doesn't," Seth replied. "It's just crazy to me how it seems to have come out of nowhere, though. It's nuts. But I guess that doesn't matter. I'll just say it. The safest thing would probably be to just get a room for the night and finish the drive tomorrow, don't you think? I mean, what's one more night, anyway?"

"Yeeaahhhh," Katie said, frustrated but also knowing Seth was right.

"Besides, if we were to keep driving, storm or no, by the time we get to Charleston it'll be too late to do anything other than sleep. Might as well get there well rested, especially if the alternative is pushing through and potentially ending up in a wreck."

"I know, I know." She swiped the screen on her phone again, unlocking it. "Well, I guess I'll look for a ... oh yeah, I guess I *can't* look for a hotel. No service."

"Yeah. That's no fun, huh?"

"How are we supposed to find a room, then?"

Seth let out a laugh. "Are you serious?"

Katie sat there, a confused look on her face.

"Katie, for God's sake, woman. I'll just go back in and ask the people at this diner if there's a hotel here. You're a child of the 90s; you were around before all this fancy technology. Use your brain!"

Katie's face fell flat, her eyes narrowing. "Shut up."

A bright flash shot across the sky as another bolt of lightning illuminated the darkness, followed by another rumble of thunder and the heavy splats of a steady rain against the vehicle.

"Looks like it's arrived."

"Yeah," Seth said. "Guess I better go before it gets too bad. Don't worry, I'll be quick." He leaned over and kissed her. "Lock the doors! Don't want any crazies trying anything." He laughed, then opened the door and headed across the lot toward the diner.

The rain pelted Seth good as he crossed the lot. He ran for the door, hoping to get inside quickly, but when he placed his hand on the doorhandle and pulled, it wouldn't budge. Caught off guard, he looked through the glass and saw several patrons and workers inside, going just as they had been a few minutes before. He pulled again, but the door wouldn't budge.

"Hey," he called out, waving his hands to get someone's attention.

An older woman walked over and stood in front of the door. "Can I help you?" she said.

Seth stood there in shock. "Can I come in? It's pouring rain!"

The woman was still for a moment, her eyebrows furrowing as she weighed the decision. She leaned over and saw their SUV in the lot. "You had the young woman with you, right?"

"What? Uh, I mean, yes, Katie. That's my wife. Why?"

The old woman walked over to one of the windows in the diner and peered out, looking around the dark lot as if expecting to see someone lurking there in the rain.

"Listen," Seth yelled out, "I just need directions. I'm not a lunatic or anything. Can you please let me in? I'm getting soaked to the bone out here!"

The old woman slowly made her way back to the door and looked in Seth's eyes. "I'll unlock the door and let you in, but only for a minute. Long enough for you to get what you need and be on your way. Your wife shouldn't be left alone in this storm. Make it quick, yeah?"

Seth arched back, taken by surprise at what the old woman said. "Yeah, sure, whatever, just let me in!"

The woman nodded and opened the door, her face showing concern. "Come on in and make it quick. Your wife shouldn't be left alone ... not in *this* storm, and certainly not tonight." As Seth stepped into the diner, the old woman stuck her head out the door and took a final look around the lot.

"Wow, this is certainly different." Seth looked around the diner. It was as if time had stopped; everyone was still, silent, and they all stared at him.

"Okay, young man, what is it you need?"

"Oh, uhm, well, we, my wife, Katie, and I, pulled off the interstate to eat. That's why we were here earlier. You see, we're headed to Charleston for a wee—"

"Do you need directions back to the interstate? Is that what this is?" The woman looked out the door again, keeping an eye on their SUV.

"Well, uh, no. We figured it safest to just stay the night here and wait out the storm. We lost cell service, and we were just wondering if you could give us directions to the nearest hotel."

The woman sighed. Her hands shook a bit, her uncomfortableness with everything happening evident. "I think it would be best if you all headed back to the interstate and just went on your way. But if you *must*, there's a hotel a couple miles on down the road. Just turn left and drive until you see it on the right."

Seth smiled, unsure of whether or not he should be offended. "I'm sorry, but *what?* Is there something wrong, or ..."

The woman looked out the door again, scanning the entire lot. "Listen," she said, taking in deep, weary breath. "Most days, *any* day other than this, actually, there wouldn't be an issue. Tonight, however, is *not* the time to visit Saint Star."

"Just tonight, huh? Is there something particularly *bad* about tonight in general that I should know about?"

The old woman turned and looked him dead in the eyes. "Yes, there is. Tonight's the night that *she* comes back."

Seth squinted, the smallest hint of a grin forming. "*She?* She who?"

"The *witch* of Dix River Swamp. That's *who*!"

Seth was silent for a moment, the words registering in his mind. After a few seconds, though, he burst out laughing. He couldn't help it. What was he supposed to do, after all? Be afraid of a *witch?*

"Okkkaaaaayyyy?"

The old woman's expression unchanged, she grabbed Seth by the arm. "You listen, and you listen *good*! You've already been here five minutes too long, so I'll make it quick."

Seth stood there, listening intently while at the same time trying not to laugh and make a joke of the whole thing, as the woman gave him the abbreviated version of the legend of the Dix River Swamp Witch.

Back in the SUV, Katie watched Seth run through the parking lot toward the diner as rain dumped on him.

"Watch out for the *crazies*, huh?" she said. "The only crazy person here is *you*, dear." She opened a game on her phone and tried fitting an assortment of blocks into various spots in order to fill entire rows and clear them from the screen, but that particular level was giving her issues. "Great," she said, swiping up and closing the game out of frustration.

The rain was heavy and steady, with each strong gust of wind pushing sheets of rain against the vehicle. Several paths of water formed on the windshield as raindrops accumulated and ran together, obscuring her view. Across the lot, she could see tree limbs swaying back and forth in the light of a streetlamp at the edge of the road. Lightning flashed, once again brightening the night sky. It was beautiful, regardless of everything else. There was just something about a good storm, something that was hard to explain, something that brought her a feeling of joy.

Katie leaned her head against the window and stared at the tree line next to the road. The way the branches swayed in the wind almost seemed intentional, as if they were doing a dance meant just for her, a dance meant for her own personal entertainment. She moved her head back and forth with them, trying to mimic each intricate movement of the leaves. It made her smile, the thought that the trees were doing that just for her.

Lightning flashed again, but something else caught her attention this time.

A shadow, something *just* outside the reach of the

streetlamp's light.

Katie pulled her head away from the window and stared out into the night. It was impossible to see through the darkness and the rain, but there had been something there, or at least she thought there had. Something, or someone, maybe? She shook her head and forced a laugh.

No, she thought. *Something, maybe, but not someone. Why would someone, anyone, actually, be out there right now? They'd have to be crazy to be standing out in the middle of a parking lot in a storm like this.*

She stared hard, and the trees continued to dance, swaying to and fro in the storm. There was nothing there that she could see, and in her mind, she knew that had to be the case. It was only logical. It had to have been her mind playing tricks on her, making her see things in the shadows, the darkness, the storm.

It was just the lightning, that was all. Just the way the lightning made it loo–

Another lightning bolt shot across the horizon.

Katie gasped and jumped as the figure came into view again, and this time there was no question. It was darker than the surrounding night, nothing more than an out-of-place shadow, really, and in her mind, she knew it was probably just a tree stump or maybe a garbage can or something of the like. And the fact that it had been visible for less than a second, only showing against the flash of light from the storm, made it less likely, but for that split second, Katie would have sworn there was a person standing there.

She forced a laugh, but it wasn't her normal laugh. It was high-pitched, her nerves on edge. *There's no way that was a—*

Lightning cut through the night again, the dark

parking lot illuminated as bright as day. She saw it clearly—a figure, a small woman, a child maybe, standing there in the pouring rain. They were closer, maybe fifty feet out. A cold chill ran down Katie's spine, and her hands began to shake. There *was* someone out there, she was certain of it. She saw them with her own eyes this time.

A million questions ran rampant through her mind. *Who* was it? *Why* were they there? Were they in trouble? Were they in danger?

A shot of adrenaline coursed through her veins; her stomach lurched up into her chest as another thought came crashing down on her.

What if they're a danger to me?

Her heart pounded, blood pumping through her body so fiercely it felt as though her flesh was on fire. Her hands shook violently as a cascade of endorphins spilled into her bloodstream. She was afraid. She was truly afraid.

Her mind went in a million directions, her hands moving frantically to find the lock on the door. Her eyes were fixed on the spot she last saw whoever or whatever it was out there, but it was still just on the outer edge of the radius covered by the streetlamp. It was almost as if that person, that *thing*, or whatever it was, knew to stay hidden.

Her hand found something on the door, a button maybe, a lever. It didn't matter; her only thought was to get the fucking door locked. Out of sheer panic and without thought, her fingers wrapped around the object and pressed. It didn't move. Her attention was still on that spot in the rain, her gaze piercing into the darkness with intense focus. Again she pushed down, but nothing happened. She grabbed the object tighter and felt movement.

Another push, nothing.

A pull.

Ah! That's it! she thought. *Now it's—*

But that wasn't it, not at all.

Something had happened, yes, but it wasn't what she intended. A sudden rush of cold air whistled around her shoulder, her neck. Something frigid and wet dripped down onto her hand, and she knew in that instant what she had done. The object in her hand hadn't been the lock, it had been the doorhandle, and she had pulled with just enough force to crack the door slightly open.

She gasped as the cold air from outside filled her lungs. Thunder exploded, and lightning filled the night sky, streaks scattering left and right like a braided stream channel down a steep mountain slope. And there, in front of her, nose pressed to the outside of the passenger-side window, was a woman.

Katie screamed and jumped back, her hip crashing into the center console hard. She shook her head, closed her eyes tight, and forced them open again, hoping the woman would be gone, a figment of her imagination. But it wasn't so. She was still there, and something about her didn't look quite right.

A smile stretched across the woman's lips that seemed too large to fit her face, almost as if it started in the opening of one ear, ripping and severing gray-toned skin before reaching the opposite ear. Blood dripped down her chin, covering yellow-stained teeth. The entire appearance of the woman reminded Katie of a description she had read of Death. Her hair, what little she had, grew from random patches of what appeared to be crusted-over scabs atop her scalp, each rain-soaked strand lying draped across her face, clinging to her nose and cheeks like half-rotted flesh peeling away from bone.

Her breath held, Katie froze in disbelief as she stared into the woman's eyes—eyes that were nothing more than empty, soulless voids of inky darkness. "N-no," Katie managed. "Le-lea-leave me alone!" She started crying hysterically, her mind scrambling for a way out of this horror. "Seth!" she shouted. "Seth! Please help me!"

Without flinching, the woman raised both hands and placed them on the edge of the door. It was still ajar, not fully open but not really closed. She scratched at the windows with long, frail fingernails, tapping them on the glass as if taunting a child.

Katie screamed again as tears flowed down her face like a leaky faucet. "Please, just leave me alone!"

The woman outside shook her head slowly, and somehow, her smile grew even larger. She ran her fingers around the edges of the door, placing them through the tiny crack. One by one, her fingers flattened and turned limp like Fettuccine noodles, sliding into the vehicle before inflating to normal thickness again. As they thickened, they lengthened, too, growing to at least ten feet in length.

Like thin, fleshy tendrils from hell, the woman's noodle-like fingers stretched toward Katie, wrapping around her arms and legs. She fought with everything she had, but no matter how hard she kicked, no matter how hard she punched, no matter how hard she ripped at the finger noodles, it was no use. Each time Katie thought she had two in her grip, four more crept from around and beneath her, wrapping her up and squeezing her limbs, her chest, forcing precious air from her lungs. She tried to scream again, but it wasn't possible to scream if she couldn't fill her lungs, and the woman's fingers had a firm hold around her chest.

Unable to scream, Katie watched in horror as the woman's mouth opened wide, each side of her jaw working independently as if it had been purposefully dislocated. From inside, a tongue appeared, moving about and slithering like a serpent as it lengthened and found its way into the crack in the door. Katie tried to move, to break free one final time, but it was impossible.

The woman's tongue snaked its way into the door crack, flickering against any section of Katie's bare skin it could find, eventually creeping its way into her mouth and down her throat.

Katie wanted to vomit, but she couldn't even breathe. She could feel it as it slid around in her mouth like a slimy worm, dancing over her teeth, her tongue, her tonsils, until it forced its way past the epiglottis and into her esophagus. She gagged hard, her eyes tearing up even more. Her vision blurred, and the last thing she saw before blacking out was the horrid face of the thing outside.

Seth had only been gone for around ten minutes, but by the time he got back to the vehicle, the storm was in full rage. "Holy shit," he said, getting inside the SUV and slamming the door. "I don't know what's crazier—this storm or the people who live in this town! I swear, they wouldn't stop talking about some local legend, something about a witch in the swamp and how it relates to this kind of storm. Like I give a fuck about all that. Hell, they even tried to convince me to just keep driving!"

He glanced over to the passenger seat and saw Katie there, curled up in a ball. She was asleep. He smiled and nodded. "Seems about right. I finally heard a good story, and I can't even tell it to you." He reached over and shook her lightly. "Katie, wake up. I got directions to a—"

"No!" she screamed, a sudden jerk as she flung her arm to the side. "Leave me *alone*!" Her arm flailed again, the bottom of her fist making contact with Seth's face.

"Fuck me!" he yelled, arching back and grabbing his face. "What the *fuck*, Katie?"

"No, no! Leave me alo-" She raised up, eyes springing open as she looked around the SUV. "Wh-where is she? Where did she go?"

"You busted my fucking nose, Katie!" he yelled out, pinching the bridge of his nose to try to slow the bleeding. "What the fuck? Reach me some napkins out of the glove compartment."

"What? Wh-what happened?" She looked around the vehicle frantically, but there was no woman, no tentacled noodle fingers, no serpent-like tongue slipping down her gullet. Her hands found her throat as she gagged.

"What's got into you?" Seth said.

Katie turned and looked at him. Blood dripped down his chin and onto his shirt. "Oh, did I ... I-I mean, I'm sorry, Seth. I must've had a bad dream, I guess. Yeah, it was a—"

"Reach me some napkins, for god's sake. I'm bleeding out over here."

She grabbed a handful of napkins from the glove compartment and handed them over. "I'm so sorry, I just thou–"

"What? That I was trying to kill you? I'm telling you,

that's almost as crazy as what happened in the diner."

"No, well, y-yeah, I guess. I mean, I thought you were this, I don't know. It just seemed so real." She looked at him again, reaching her hand out to touch his leg. "I'm so sorry, Seth."

"Yeah, yeah. It's fine. Just busted, I think. But goddamn, girl. You decked me good. Man, *fuck* this night."

She apologized again, but there was nothing that could be done about it at that point.

Seth knew she hadn't meant to hit him, but that didn't change the fact that it hurt like hell. It took less than five minutes for him to stop the bleeding, and once he wiped off as best he could, they headed down the road to find the hotel.

The storm was strong, wind and rain whipping and falling like crazy as Seth did his best to stay between the faded lines on the road. Not only was there a literal monsoon going on, but a thick fog somehow managed to creep in while it was downpouring.

Katie leaned back in her seat, trying to calm down. "Wow, where did all this fog come from?"

"Well, probably the swamp that surrounds this town."

"Huh? A swamp?"

"Yep, or at least that's what the lady back there at the diner told me. And *boy*, did she have a story to go with it."

Katie shifted in her seat a bit. She suddenly felt uncomfortable, a faint sensation of nausea swirling in her stomach. "Yeah?" She tried to stay interested, but she was having trouble paying attention.

"Ooohhhh yeah. The lady there said that tonight was not a good night to be here because of it. But the craziest part is that she said this was an annual storm, a storm that had been coming on this exact same day every year for the last several hundred years."

"Huh," Katie said, the feeling in her stomach getting worse.

"Yeah, and brace yourself for the kicker, because it's nuts. The whole reason it started, according to the lady and every other loon in that diner, was because the ancestors of Saint Star killed a witch that used to live in this swamp. Apparently, it's called the Dix River Swamp, and they call the witch the Dix River Swamp Witch, and this storm is supposedly some kind of ritual or something, I guess. Hell, they didn't even want to let me in the diner again!"

"Witch?" she murmured, her stomach growing queasier with every second. "What about a witch?" Memories of the woman at the window flashed in her mind, and the word *witch* suddenly hit in a very dark and familiar way.

"Yeah. I guess this storm comes on the same day every year, and it brings the witch back with it, or she brings it with her when she comes. I'm not really sure of the specifics, I was just trying to get out of there. They weren't necessarily the nicest or most polite folks, if you know what I mean."

Katie wanted to listen, wanted to hear about the witch, but the sick feeling in her stomach took precedence over everything else. All she could focus on was trying not to vomit. The driving was making it worse, and on top of that, she was getting dizzy too. Her head felt like what she expected living inside a snow globe would feel like if someone shook it, and it intensified the nausea.

"Anyway, from what I could gather, this day all those years back is the same day they hanged her, and for whatever reason, this is her way of trying to come back."

Katie was trying her hardest to pay attention and hear what Seth was saying, but the sickness was too overwhelming. It was more than that, though. She felt off, unlike herself. It was like she was changing, or something inside her was. She closed her eyes, pinching them shut hard. Her stomach turned, her heart raced, beads of sweat formed on her forehead and face, and a flash of heat radiated to the top of her skin. She opened her eyes, and everything around her started spinning. Up moved down, left moved right, even sitting down she could find no balance, and she was certain she was going to pass out.

"It's like they still live in the olden times. Isn't that crazy?" he continued, his primary focus still set on not running off the road. "Folks down here still believin' in witches and the like? I mean, come on! I guess we really are in the middle of bumfuck nowhere, huh? Hell, Katie, they even said something about fertilizing a demon or some shit. Told me you shouldn't be left alone in this storm because she may try to use you as a vessel to get what she wants."

For a brief moment, a surge of pure fear crept up from deep inside her, but just as fast as it showed itself, the feeling disappeared, taken over by anger, rage, and excitement all at once. A bright wave of light flashed in her vision, robbing her of sight. She panicked at first, a sharp gasp, but after only a second or two, the lights vanished and a sudden calm fell over her.

She wasn't sure what was happening inside herself, but she knew it felt good. She knew she *liked* it.

Seth turned to her slowly, both concerned and curious about the noise she just made. Was she crying? Had he said something to upset her? "Katie, are you okay?"

She sat up as she stared straight through the windshield out into the storm. "Yes," she said in a hushed but very matter-of-fact tone. "Why, I'm absolutely perfect."

He shot her a look, his attention split between the road and her. Something about her seemed strange. She even looked different, but he couldn't quite put his finger on how. "Okay. I just wanted to make sure. It kinda sounded like you were crying or in pain or something."

Katie was silent, her stare unflinching.

"Katie?"

Rain dumped onto the windshield; heavy gusts of wind blew water droplets sideways into the doors, peppering the entire vehicle like pellets from a shotgun.

"Katie, are you okay?"

Up ahead, a red sign flickered, cutting through the thick fog. He leaned in and squinted. "Well, it looks like this is our place."

She remained quiet, not even as much as a flinch or a blink from her as far as Seth could tell. He was getting nervous, worrying about her, not because of what the townsfolk had said but because she just didn't seem to be acting normal.

He pulled into the gravel lot of the hotel and parked in front of the main office. The red glow from the vacancy sign lit up their SUV with a neon-pink glow. "Okay, you just hang out here, and I'll run in and grab us a room. Does that wor–"

"Your cock," she said, her tone sharp and direct. "Give me your cock, *now*!"

Shocked and surprised, Seth whipped his head around. She was staring at him, a smile creeping on the edge of mischievous and evil plastered on her mouth. Her hair hung over her face, its natural red color accentuated in the glow of the light. He shook his head, slightly confused, and he couldn't help but chuckle. "Wait, what did you just say?"

"You heard me. I said, *give me your cock*!"

Seth was completely still for what seemed like minutes, his mind trying to process what his ears heard. It wasn't like her to demand such an act—she was usually *much* more reserved and conservative with such matters, *especially* being in a parking lot of a business. He angled his head to the side and grinned. "Uh ... are you being serious right now?"

Without hesitation, she lunged for him. With one arm, she pinned him back against the seat, her other hand finding and undoing his belt and the button and zipper of his jeans.

"Holy *shit*, Katie," he said, trying to raise up. Her strength was too much, though. "Can't we wait until we get to the roooommmmohmygod!"

Just as he was finishing his thought, she wrapped her warm, wet lips around the head of his limp dick. Her left hand still pressing him against the back of the seat, her right hand made its way across his thigh and under his testicles, cupping them. In one fluid motion, her head bobbed up and down as his prick stiffened.

"Whoa, Wh-what's got into *you*?" he asked, looking around nervously. The last thing he wanted was to get caught getting his cock sucked in the parking lot of the Saint Star Inn.

Katie slid her left hand down and wrapped her fingers around his shaft, stroking him as she slurped. After a few strokes, she raised her head up and took his cock from her mouth as she glanced up at him. "Gotta fertilize the demon," she said, her voice taking on a strange sort of wicked hiss.

"What … what did you just …" To Seth's surprise, her eyes had changed. They looked clouded over. The whites weren't white anymore. Instead, they were a mixture of dark grays and greens.

She slid her lips down over his member again, causing him to throw his head back in pure pleasure. Up and down, she worked to get him to the point of climax.

Seth was terribly confused, but no matter how confused he was, he knew better than to question it or say too much. His cock was in her mouth and she was sucking like a goddamn madwoman. What else was there to question? It felt amazing, after all, and honestly, there was no real point in stopping her, at least in his current state of mind.

"Oh *fuck*," he moaned. "I … I'm gonna fuckin' cum, Katie!"

Never taking his cock out of her mouth, she replied, "Down my fucking throat."

Once those mumbled words slipped from her lips, it took less than five seconds for Seth to explode. He moaned and groaned like a wild animal, thrusting his hips upward to shove his rock-hard cock as deep down her throat as he could. Thrust after thrust, pump after pump, his balls contracted, his penis throbbing as rope after rope of sticky, wet semen pumped into her mouth and down her gullet.

As his dick stopped throbbing and started losing its erection, he took in one deep and lasting breath, then exhaled. "Holy motherfuck," he groaned, his muscles relaxing into a heap in the driver's seat. "That felt amazing."

Katie sat up straight and swallowed hard. "Gotta fertilize the demon."

"Huh?"

"Gotta fertilize the demon," she repeated, her voice slightly higher in pitch. "Fertilize the demon. Fertilize the demon. And now gotta *feed* it!"

He looked over at her, his limp muscles all but useless. "What are you talkin' about?"

Like a starved beast, she jumped toward him, her mouth going directly for his limp dick. In one fluid motion, she grabbed his balls, shoved her face down hard over his flaccid member, and closed her mouth, clamping her teeth together like a steel bear trap.

Seth let out a scream like no other, its sharpness piercing into the night to near glass-breaking frequencies. "What the *fuuuucccckkkk*!"

She raised her head up from his lap and smiled. Blood dripped down her chin, and she fiddled with something in her cheek pouch.

A horrid sensation turned Seth's stomach as he continued to scream. "Fuuuuccccckkkkk!"

He grabbed for the handle and flung the door open, spilling out into the rain. His groin pulsed with pain. He looked up and saw the main office. "Help me!" he cried out. "Please, someone help me!"

Katie walked around and stood in front of him. "Fertilize the demon, then feed it. Now let it out." She took a couple steps back and lurched, dry heaving like a cat readying itself to vomit.

Seth cried hysterically. He was confused, in pain, bleeding from his severed penis stump, and all he wanted to do was get the fuck out of there.

She lurched again, and suddenly, he saw a large protuberance in her abdomen. It moved every time she heaved, up to her chest, then her throat, and finally stalling for a second at her mouth.

"What the ... fucking *help* me! Someone, *please*!"

As he watched, two red hands emerged from her mouth, breaking her jawbone in the process. Shortly after, an elbow forced its way up, then a shoulder, and before he knew it, he was watching a small person crawl out of her body.

He screamed again, and though Seth wasn't a praying man, he fucking prayed.

He saw the little man more than halfway out of her face, and he let out another cry.

Out of nowhere, a loud explosion echoed in the night, and the head of the man emerging from Katie's mouth burst into a slurry of blood and bone, spraying all over Seth. He heard the faint sound of a gun cocking, and another blast rang out, followed by the explosion of Katie's head.

Her knees buckled, and her body fell to the ground, along with the remains of the little man halfway out of her throat. Behind them, standing tall in the glow of the vacancy sign, stood a man sporting a twelve-gauge shotgun.

"Sorry about that, mister," the man said to Seth. "Diana called me from the diner a little while ago. She said a couple outta towners were headed my way. Looks like the ol' witch done got to your wife, huh?"

Seth lay there, blank-faced, squeezing his dick nub to try to stop the bleeding.

"Well, I'll be goddamned. It looks like she bit your pecker off too." The old man bared his teeth and winced. "'At's a fuckin' shame. I guess I'll call you an ambulance. Give 'em a few minutes and they'll come get you. Just try to keep steady pressure on it. Wouldn't want you to bleed out on me, now."

Rain poured onto Seth as his vision faded in and out.

The last thing he saw before passing out was the man with the shotgun, the very man who had saved his life and killed his wife, walk back into the office.

Dead Water

K.K. Monroe

No place tried to kill a person as much or as often as the wilds of Louisiana did. The wetlands were part of his fabric, and bad memories had a way of stirring awake the dead.

A ghost or two accompanied Remi as he stepped down from the dock onto the awaiting airboat. The palpable miasma of bittersweet recollections slipped over his disquieted thoughts like a heavy mourner's cowl woven from scratchy emotions, stitched together by intrusive thoughts and invasive reminders. The weight and texture of it made his brain itch.

Theo Lejeune ran a small outfit of swamp boats in the remote Noiret Parish.

Lanky, tanner than a roasted chestnut, with more rawhide than meat, the captain awaited him onboard. "Been too long, Ti-Remi," Theo said in a solemn, quiet greeting.

At six feet tall, the affectionate moniker for children

Ti no longer fit his size or age, yet that didn't dissuade the gray-whiskered Cajun from using it. Remi was Dr. Thibodeaux, Forensic Pathologist badge swinging from a lanyard around his neck.

"You done good for yourself." Theo flicked the laminated badge with his grimy fingers. Dark, brooding eyes studied Remi with a mixture of tainted nostalgia and a touch of pride. "*Mais* ... you shouldn't have come back here."

A pregnant pause hung between them, like a tied sack full of squirming worms.

Neither man dared to cut the bait bag open to see what spilled out.

"Wasn't by my choice," Remi admitted with a grimace. Detoured from his usual assistant-coroner duties in Orleans parish, his boss had forced him two hours south central to the Atchafalaya Basin, then farther south, deep into the watershed.

There would be no *fais-do-do* for this particular reunion, no lively Acadian music or exuberant zig-zagging to Dewey Balfa's legendary music, no tapping of heels keeping beat with the percussive tangs of gilded fiddlesticks as they danced the night away like they once had.

Chagrined, Remi met Theo's gaze for the briefest of moments.

That was the look he hated most—the pitying look.

"Where's everyone else at?" Remi asked.

"They've gone out already, got here before even the crazy roosters could *cocorico*." Theo hocked up phlegm and spit the wad over the side. "I wanted to take you out myself."

"Where we headed?" Remi didn't know details other than there was a suspicious death, and the sole coroner who covered the isolated parish was out on emergency leave.

"Dead Water Swamp."

Theo's reply dropped Remi's insides a hundred floors in under three seconds, stomach stuck to the roof of his mouth.

He swallowed hard as Theo ran a hand through his thick, wavy, salt-and-pepper hair, sun-cracked lips puckering like ass ends of a sausage. "Dat's the worst we've ever had," Theo announced before abruptly ball-capping his handiwork.

Unhealed wounds festered, leaked vitriol, the bark erupting like a mad dog. "You sure about that?" He hadn't intended to bark. The past wasn't Theo's fault.

"Ti-Remi," Theo lamented soulfully, "a different kind of worse."

Eighteen years had passed since they last saw each other. Theo looked to have aged twice that in the span. "What happened ... how ... what you thought you saw?" Theo stumbled over his words, kicking at proverbial rocks, then took a deep breath and pronounced, "What the swamp takes, it doesn't give back." Sage as ever, the captain left the rest of the horror show unspoken.

Better that way.

Besides, it was too fucking hot to revisit how, after; teenage Remi took a one-way trip to the mental hospital for an extended six-month stay. Primordial swamp soup brewed horrors which defied human comprehension, yet not a single, local soul had believed a word he said.

Psychotic break secondary to PTSD. They were fancy words to excuse the bullshit.

Back then, Remi had waited for Theo and Eula to come for him. When they hadn't, as a juvenile with no living blood relatives, the state put him into the care system. He was much more fortunate than most under the circumstances, at least in regards to foster care, which worked out in its own way and provided him opportunities the swamp life couldn't.

Remi stayed away from the sunken edges of the airboat. Swamp-butt heat, a muggy, oily residue thicker and fouler than sweat, slicked his skin. Protective work clothing exponentially multiplied the intensity of the balmy ninety-degree weather. A plethora of pockets in the navy sports pants held backup field supplies, mostly a pair of tweezers, a penlight, extra baggies of sterile gloves, and, just in case, a saw-toothed hunting knife slipped inside the deepest pocket.

Drenched by sweat, wet patches spread across his broad chest. Growing puddles darkened along his back, wet rings underscoring both armpits. The tall, state-issued, bright-yellow waders created an additional, insufferable layer of insulation, steaming him alive in the infamous Cajun boil. In an instant, a dense cloud of mosquitos swarmed him.

The hellacious, whining, backwater minions resembled large flies.

Needing the blood to feed their eggs, only female mosquitos would attack. Frenzied by bloodlust, like piranhas in heat, the she-devils converged upon him at once. Sharp as sewing needles, countless proboscises pierced clothing and his skin, gorging on succulent blood. Swollen bug bites spread in a rash of itchy, pink pox.

Years of conditioning gave Remi the advantage of resisting the amygdala's hardwired impulse to freak out. Swatting and smacking would serve no purpose.

Swamp-bred *maringouin* were engineered to fight back.

Undeterred by another heavier fogging of deet repellent, the ravenous drove of insects breached the sensitive perimeter of his external ear canal. Ticking veins in his throat acted as ripened fruit nectar, while mutated acoustics—propellered airplane arriving and departing the same landing pad, simultaneously—intensified inside his skull in a familiar lullaby of misery.

It was one he used to fall asleep to, surrounded by Papaw's collection of gator skulls.

His gaze drifted from the stowed gear to the bayou's murky, black waters.

Ghostly-gray Spanish moss draped from bald cypresses in ominous spidery veils, twisted tree trunks propped up by bulbous protrusions above the bayou's slow-moving current. Harsh environments demanded peculiar adaptations for survival, and the mud-drenched roots had evolved into knobby knuckles and knotty kneecaps jutting above the waterline in order to breathe. Primeval forests attested to how alien lifeforms emerged, shaped by the demands of hostile environments and thrived despite them.

The engine roared to life, drowning out the incessant buzzing of attacking insects.

Headed into a labyrinthine maze of creeping marshland, sunlight dappled Remi's face. The bayou swallowed the glaring sun, then the entire sky as a primeval forest sank them into a world of shadows.

At the sound of the approaching engine, a blue heron lifted from marsh grass.

An assembly line of turtles tumbled from a log into tannin waters.

The swift breeze ushered the biting minions back to hell.

Attraper des gros oua-oua-rons, *Ti-Remi,* the ghost of memory rattled off excitedly in his ear, urging the scrawny boy from long ago to hunt and capture hefty frogs.

Catching and gigging fat summer bullfrogs and pig frogs with Papaw from the pirogue were some of Remi's fondest childhood memories. At the momentary lifting of his mood, a ghastly vision of prehistoric jaws rose from the nether of remote memory. A ten-footer, at least, stealthily emerged from the swamp's inky depths and stalked them, undetected.

What was a floating log wasn't a floating log at all.

Papaw's face was turned toward teenage Remi, his only grandson, his *cher,* smiling out from those remarkably large, nicotine-stained teeth. Just as Papaw leaned over to rinse frog slime from his hands in turbid waters, the *Cocodrie* opened its hungry jaws and lunged with breakneck speed. The merciless apex predator latched onto both forearms. Papaw cried out as massive razored teeth snapped, cracking his bones with hard snaps. Ropy muscles with green-sleeved, taloned feet lifted from the burbling agitation of sulfuric water. Sticky, greenish-yellow algae floated out from scutes on the reptile's massive head.

Peach skin dripped with slime and sludge.

An amalgam of human appendages mixed with deadly gator parts seized Papaw by the waddle of the throat, his gray tufts of hair puffed out with fright. Crisscrossed wrinkles of badly sun-damaged skin smoothed into a mask of undiluted terror, forever memorialized by

Remi's psyche as a living nightmare. The monstrosity snatched Papaw from the pirogue.

A wheezing rattle, a final gasp, emitted from Papaw's ghastly, terror-awed rictus.

Screaming wildly, teenage Remi swiped an oar, and the pirogue rocked dangerously, threatening to spill him into the perilous waters beside Papaw and the behemoth. He pummeled dirty water with the oar, unable to strike close enough to the creature to land a blow. Not that it would have mattered, for he was helpless to do anything but watch the killing machine drag the man he loved, both a surrogate Papa and Maman, under the water.

The *Cocodrie* toyed with its prey. Gator jaws weren't designed to chew but for swallowing food whole. The creature flounced Papaw, as frail and limp as a broken ragdoll. Flesh slapped against the water like a wet towel against the floor.

Then the gargantuan beast began a death roll.

Rather than spinning forcefully to shear off manageable hunks to eat, the hunter luxuriated in the kill, rolling and rolling with sheer amphibious prowess and brutality, intent on drowning its prey. Papaw didn't stand a chance or put up any fight.

Under and over, Remi watched in horror as Papaw appeared then disappeared, tears cascading down his face. Hoarsened by the uncontrollable shrieking, his voice croaked every time the *Cocodrie's* pale belly flashed above the surface.

Until the waters eventually stilled, turning blacker and more rufescent than dried blood.

The gator took Papaw under, stuffed his body beneath an underwater log or in some watery hole, to tenderize the meat for later consumption, leaving Remi with only the horrid memory of it. The toxic trauma of watching someone a person loves dearly die horribly right before their broken eyes left insidious scars. Prowling grief pounced when he least expected, thoughts and emotions fracturing into a million reflective shards of cutting guilt, shame, and regret.

He had no one left in the black-hearted bayou to summon him home. Venturing into the eerie desolation of Black Bayou, where it all happened, Remi sensed the cold-blooded monster out there somewhere, lurking beneath the surface. Foreboding told him to turn back.

He knew what he saw—a thing not quite human, not quite alligator.

The abomination haunted him.

"It wasn't *Cocodrie*," teenage Remi told them, trembling and shaking in shock as paramedics from a distant parish bundled him up. "It had human hair, human forearms, crooked, human-like elbows. I tell you, it was an actual Swamp Monster!"

Muggy sweat turned cold, trickling down from his suprasternal notch, and an icy fingernail scraped a trail of grief on the way to Remi's damaged heart.

Yet there was Papaw, a scruffy, aged specter seated at the bow of the roaring airboat. The specter tipped a reddened face back, releasing a gleeful howl. "Ayeeeeeeeee!"

The Cajun call of excitement, the sincerest form of celebration from a rich syncretic heritage, flared painfully, excavating an existential wound the size of a boulder from his pounding chest cavity. *Ayeeeeeeeee* skimmed across verdant-green top skin, like a stone skipping across time. Grief hallucinations, or whatever they were, peeled back edges of the bleakness enshrouding him. Though he felt mad, seeing and hearing Papaw's *esprit* somehow dampened the swamp stench of sun-rotten eggs and vegetal decomposition.

The slow-moving bayou narrowed to a stagnant neck, crossing dead water. They moved deeper into the murk. Ten minutes later, Theo killed the engine.

And the specter was gone.

Shadows blurred any distinguishable margins of Dead Water Swamp's sprawling shoreline. From within the uncanny gloaming of twilight, though it was early morning beyond the interior, the hanging corpse's pale flesh illuminated like moonglow.

While he sat in silence staring at the body, blood-sucking vortexes engulfed him.

"When was she found?" he finally asked the three men seated on a second airboat.

"Yesterday afternoon," replied a man younger even than Remi, introducing himself as Dante, a forensic tech dispatched from Baton Rouge, prominent Adam's apple bobbing hard.

Whoever committed the atrocity against the naked woman had wrapped her in braided chains, hung her upside down, then hoisted her up in an ancient cypress like a sow for slaughter. Her head was submerged in impenetrable brackish water beneath a buttressed trunk, her flounced arms revealed contusions, gouges, and gashes, and the waterline was above the wrists.

"Chicken-necking for crabs," Barnabé commented churlishly, sucking a boiled peanut between his teeth before spitting the empty shell into a cup. "Tied her up like raw chicken bait." A crude analogy Remi didn't care for, he found the NOLA detective wasn't wrong.

Red mudbugs trawled the bruised-purple lividity of the torso, scavenging flesh.

At the sight of the carrion feeders, typical nightly fare, Theo's face sank with a look of utter revulsion. Barnabé stood, thumping his barrel chest with restless energy. Leroy, the second captain, eyed the Glock hanging from a belt slung around the detective's hip like a gunslinger and decided against speaking whatever evident unpleasantry had come to mind.

"We're sick of waiting on you," Barnabé complained loudly after a final thump.

From a distance, Remi carried on studying the corpse, unbothered by the scowling Creole with muscular tree trunks for thighs. "Who discovered her way out here?"

Barnabé was a gym monkey, pumping iron to thwart dry-drunk stress, a hothead Remi had crossed paths with plenty in NOLA. He exclaimed, "I got that information already, *couillon*!"

"Who you calling *couillon*?!" Theo started at the affront. "I'll put the *gris-gris* on you."

"Dis here backs up to Rue des Fleurs pour les Morte," Leroy smoothly interjected, surprise flickering in Remi's eyes at the similarity to another notorious tract for body dumps nowhere near Noiret. "Voodoo Maman lives close by," he continued. "Her boys were frogging in a ditch, said a wild gator fight broke out, brought dem boys running to catch the action."

Leroy pointed out a surprisingly nearby patch of ocher-hued reeds. "Saw her from der."

Something thudded against the bottom, a dull, metallic thump from an underwater log or debris. Remi motioned for Dante, the Nikon DLSR camera hanging from a strap around his neck.

Leroy maneuvered closer for the tech to step aboard.

"Did anyone touch anything at all?" Remi pressed the group. Contamination of an active crime scene was his primary concern, especially in a highly dynamic swampland where preservation of evidence against elements and native animals proved nearly impossible.

"Refused to drive them over," Leroy replied stoically, God bless the man.

"Get us in as close as possible," Remi told Theo, snapping on sterile gloves. No way would he step foot in dead water, which while stagnant and hypoxic to varying degrees nonetheless teamed with extensive biodiverse swamp life.

All matter of aliens with claws and teeth lived beneath and above.

Remi coached Dante on which wide lens and micro shots he especially wanted.

"I know what to do," Dante offered politely, green to the gills. "I haven't seen anything like this before, and I've removed a man's hand from a blender with a spoon after his wife hit the switch. It's not like I haven't seen ... bad things." The glugging Adam's apple betrayed his uncertainty. "But this is ... next level brutality." Dante stared at Remi expectantly.

"No one's ever prepared for anything like this." Remi clapped a hand on Dante's shoulder. "But don't vomit on evidence, please," he cautioned softly.

Forty-five minutes later, Remi began the preliminary physical examination of the body. Crouched, he reached over, and Papaw's face the moment the monster crunched him up like a brittle pinecone swam into his vision. Tentatively, he reached down into the water, palpated a jutting clavicle, discovering ragged, sheared flesh.

Something nibbled on his gloves.

Startled, Remi gasped and jerked his hands to his chest, Barnabé's chuckles and taunts carrying across the water. A fanning shadow beneath the surface glimpsed from the corner of the pathologist's eye caught the aquatic scavenger in action. With rapid, segmented snaps, the crawfish furiously backpedaled using its tail, vanishing into a noxious swirl between cradled kneecaps. Crawfish didn't nibble; they plucked, shredded, and tore their food with sharp pincers.

Or crushed prey with their toothy denticles.

Crawfish were feasting on the body underwater, destroying or ingesting potential evidence. "Dante, bag a few live ones," Remi requested. "I saw a red cooler aft."

"Won't use dat cooler for muffaletta no more," Theo grumbled over Remi's shoulder.

Remi reached back into the tepid, brackish water, placing hands under mottled shoulders, carefully sliding them closer together to support the neck before lifting up the head to see her face.

There was nothing there.

"Decapitation. You taking notes, Barnabé?"

"Like we won't notice der's no head on the slab," Barnabé rejoined sarcastically.

Palpating with the care and dexterity of a blind man, Remi angled his mouth toward the digital recorder in his front pocket before speaking. "Disarticulation. Sharp protruding cervical stalk, possibly C-7. Messy avulsions. Likely an animal attack." Remi was mindful of unexpected sharp edges, jags of bone, to avoid cutting himself.

"Guess a fancy degree's required to state the obvious," smartass said, loving to hear himself talk.

"Her head may be on the bottom. Hope you brought your mask, asshole."

"They don't pay me enough to snorkel in no swamp." Barnabé crossed his meaty arms.

Nibbling came, more insistent, and Remi snatched his hands fast. Ratty edges of rapidly decomposing skin sloughed off with the gloves, clinging to his fingertips like tattered strips of plaster of Paris. Another scavenging culprit, a sour-faced catfish, flipped its tail, and foul swamp water perfused with decompensated human flotsam splashed into Remi's mouth.

Unable to control the gag reflex, he wretched, swallowing the reflux of chicory coffee.

Something struck beneath the boat, knocking forcefully. "Hold steady." Remi wiped dribbles from his lips with the back of a clean sleeve. In one smooth, practiced motion he stripped off the gloves, turned them inside out to capture the evidence, and knotted up the makeshift bag.

Piercing shrieks launched Remi's *esprit* from his body.

Claws shrilled against aluminum, like sharp nails running down a gritty chalkboard.

He turned and saw Dante's eyes bugging out. Arced, black talons curled over the camera strap, corkscrewing it around the tech's thin neck. Waders running in place released ear-splitting squeaks, and Remi grabbed onto Dante's skinny leg, pulling against an insane amount of tension.

The tech edged over the bow of the boat on his belly.

Wailing, stuck on repeat. "What the fuck? Don't let it

eat me."

Talons drew Dante in like a powerful wench.

Humanoid arms stood in sharp contrast to the gator feet and body armored in bony plates the color of soot. The unrelenting grip felt distinctly methodical. And patient. Dante dipped toward the creature's glistening, readied mouth. Within the unnatural dimness of the swamp, reptilian eyes flared with incandescent, orange-red light, and Remi flung the lanyard from his own neck, stealing furtive glances at the minefield of *Cocodrie* eyeshine.

Flaming eyes surrounded them like fiery sunrises, rising everywhere.

Dante's terror-stricken face inched closer and closer to an eddying flotsam, those pearly-white spikes smiling out knives. The tech's wailing heightened to screams that echoed inside the creature's cavernous mouth.

Suddenly remembering what his pocket held, Remi grabbed for the serrated blade, hoping to cut Dante free. Adrenaline robbed him of dexterity, and he fumbled the knife. Once righted, he sprang forward. But he was too late.

The heel of Dante's wader disappearing beneath a cloud of bubbles.

Water erupted with a tremendous explosion, splashing across the deck.

From nowhere, Theo hurled down from the sky, almost landing on top of him.

A jarring thud scand the Cajun crashed onto his side, punching Remi in the guts. A formidable tail whipped up and over the side. The mighty appendage pummeled Theo, thumping his body like a sand bag, before it disappeared back into the swamp water like a stealthy ninja.

"Oh my God, look at that thing." Frightened shouts carried from the other boat.

Pink bubbles stretched from Theo's slackened mouth, popping and splattering blood. Feverish eyes sought Remi, and he scrambled on his knees over to the captain.

"Stay still," he urged Theo, pain stabbing Remi through the heart.

Louisiana was one huge blended family of variegated heritages, beliefs, and religions. Various cultural ingredients and levels of piquant melded together to make extraordinary mouth-watering jambalayas and gumbos. There was no flavor like it. Sticky as dirty rice and beans, despite their differences, they stuck together. Until that terrible moment, Remi had forgotten how strong the bond was between him and Theo. Theo and Papaw.

Angry tears pricked Remi's eyes. "Hang on," he pleaded. "I'll get you some help."

Silently, Remi bargained for the man's life.

With his extensive medical training, he stopped short of telling Theo he would be okay.

Placating a dying person by lying to them wasn't in Remi's wheelhouse. Already, the side of Theo's face and neck darkened with spreading bruises, indicative of active bleeding trapped beneath the skin. The cataclysmic walloping caused massive internal trauma, inevitably leading to organ failure. Theo may as well have been rolled over by a dump truck.

"Eula and I did everything we could to keep you away," Theo rasped, squeezing Remi's hand like it took everything in the world for him to hold on. "I'm sorry they took you to dat dreadful hospital." Blood gurgled inside Theo's mouth, staining his teeth like cherry soda.

"We wanted to protect you, to keep you safe."

Confusion riddled Remi's face. "I don't under—"

"Lwizyàn takes too much from us, always has. I need you to know this: we love you so very much. We always have, even if it didn't always appear that way."

At the deathbed confession, the whiskered face suddenly deflated. Unstaring eyes shook Remi all over. Bitter regret choked him, and he panted, struggling to breathe.

Shots blasted from the water. Acrid gun smoke tinged the air. Remi never imagined a man built like Barnabé could produce such a noise—squeaking and screeching like a tiny, high-pitched mouse caught by its tail in a mousetrap. The Glock emptied into the reptile's leathery chest hide in a tight grouping of smoking bullseyes.

Barnabé's finger clicked the impotent trigger still.

At least thirteen feet tall, close to twelve-hundred pounds of pure muscle, The Swamp Monster dwarfed the beefy detective. Arms and legs oddly refined and feminine possessed agility and brutal strength.

Leroy hugged the motor behind the detective, weighing unfortunate options.

With a stricken look, Remi watched as Leroy hurled himself overboard and began to paddle for shore. Shallow soon enough, he stood up and stumbled, sputtering mouthfuls of fetid water. Attempting to run along the muddy, sucking bottom, he managed a few steps before a churning current carried him swiftly into a rising tide of sunbursts.

"There's an army of gators," Remi tried to warn him. Whatever had him beneath the surface delivered him up to countless snapping jaws, and Leroy went under.

Human heels were turned back above the gloved,

webbed feet like pieces of a puzzle that didn't belong together. The behemoth balanced along a metal curl of the bow with the finesse and precision of a chilling ballerina and waved a menacing manus in Barnabé's terrified face, flexing five prominent toes, an equal number of claws. Odd buttery algae grew along the curvature of its spine to midback. Eyes widening with shock, horrifying recognition dawned, melting Remi's bones in a vat of acid.

"Papaw's Killer," he whispered to himself numbly.

Unaffected by the bullet holes, it moved toward the detective with blurring speed.

Losing his mind, Remi yelled at it, "Hey, gator! Gator, get away from him!" He beat and kicked the aluminum boat to create a huge racket, same as he was taught to do to deter a bayou bear. In the frantic commotion, he dropped the fucking knife.

Mortified, Remi watched his only weapon sink out of sight.

All hopes of survival sank with it.

Claws slashed and shredded Barnabé screaming face into a grisly pom-pom.

With a quick twist, the atrocity snapped the man's muscular neck, then tossed his body overboard. A thrashing gator war broke out over dominion. Growling, territorial gators tore the meat apart in a bloody mosh pit of visceral growls and grunts.

The Swamp Monster lifted its bludgeoned snout and yawned fiercely, releasing a feral roar. Ordinary *Cocodrie* didn't roar like CGI T-Rexes from a summer blockbuster.

Chills kissed every inch of Remi's stiffening, titanium-fused spine.

He backed away in horror as windy bellows bristled

giant rag weeds, flattening reeds to reveal a jag of shoreline. Twenty feet, maybe. It wasn't too far. Just far enough to die, instantly.

Leaping into a swamp pretty much guaranteed death, and Remi had never seen so many gators congregated in one place, as if to worship.

The abomination suddenly turned and took a flying leap toward him.

Remi screamed.

The Herculean pounce landed the cold-blooded reptile center deck. The aluminum flooring sagged beneath the massive blow, buckling Remi's knees. A sickly sweet, putrid stench of gangrenous rot washed over him.

Snarling, The Swamp Monster stalked him.

Reptilian feet scratched up over the sides. Claws shrilled on aluminum, driving metal stakes into his skull. Two more creatures came onto the airboat. Claws held Theo's still-warm corpse between the abysmal amalgam of limbs. The creatures pulled fast and hard, tearing Theo's body in half, then scooped and shoveled bloody guts and shit into their chuted throats.

Unhinged screams rose and fell from Remi's burning throat. Breaths shivered his chest.

With the behemoth snapping and hissing directly above his head, Remi fell to all fours. Like a terrified child trying to outrace a boogeyman in the closet, he scurried around the console to the captain's chair, snagging an object underhand. Dumbly, Remi stared at the item in his hand.

Theo's bloodstained ball cap.

Gritty mosquitos, the tangy taste of copper from an inadvertent mastication of insects, clung to Remi's tongue in a lumpy gruel tasting of an imminent future.

Creepy, growly rumbles shorted out his overtaxed nervous system and jolted Remi into a peculiar state of semi-paralysis, fizzing with shaken, bottled-up carbonation.

Shocked awareness filtered through a hazy bloodshot film, like the lit match viewed through oleaginous glass, wavering, desperate for more oxygen. His mind revolted, unwittingly deciphering words from a grotesquerie of human language and speech.

The Swamp Monster's esophageal regurgitations of air popped like fry oil when it said, "Come willingly."

Remi forced himself to look up at the ghastly beast.

Blazing mirrors reflected back his bloodless, pinched face, hot foulness fanning his sunken cheeks. Theo's blue cap gripped to his chest, Remi matched the predator's infernal gaze in a final act of defiance to honor those it had taken. Maintaining eye contact, his thumb pressed the starter button, fingers sharply twisted the ignition key, and the engine roared to life.

Remi shouted, "Go back to Hell!" Then he flattened the throttle.

At the extreme surge in velocity, the massive creature stumbled past Remi like a drunk before tucking and performing a graceful acrobatic backflip into spraying water.

He knew then he was certifiable, a nutjob.

Like the quacks had deemed him years ago.

Careening out of his control, the airboat skimmed over increasingly shallow bogs, made a mad arc before it left the water, and crashed into wetland woods.

A mesmerizing chorus of marsh vocalizations—

Chirping crickets

Kek-kek-keking rails

Chattering kingfishers

The *hoo-kuks-fer-uuu?* of barred owls disoriented to night and day by tricky low-lighting

B*rrp-brrping* frogs and toads, vocal sacs resonating and harmonizing with the cacophony of insects

Swamp music lulled him deeper into the fugue of restful slumber.

Remi had never felt more a part of the lifeline of the bayou than at that moment. Atoms dispersed in globules of blood, streaming through the veins of a much grander organism. Unlike female mosquitos sucking on a host's blood to nourish their eggs, the bloodline fed him, and he fed it. Dreaming, drifting in a haze...

A brilliant alarm flooded through Remi on a nipping tidal wave of terror. Visions of the crew's massacre, unnatural and natural beasts comingled, the present came rushing back.

Baring his teeth, Remi snapped to an agonizing upright position, moans escaping a bloodied mouth. Bruised and battered, he struggled to stand, vaguely wondering if the damp, tangled, dusky place wasn't his crypt in the afterlife.

Waders sank, sticking in gurgling mud with each heavy, unsteady step he took.

Off to his left, tree branches snapped.

Instantly, the swamp chorus fell silent as a grave, alerting him to danger.

Throwing glances over his shoulder, Remi fled the cleaved trees and the smoldering wreckage. He navigated a dangerous, indistinct landscape of tangled vines, uplifted gnarled roots, skirting around quicksand bogs by sheer swamp instinct.

Salvation appeared like a ray of sunshine after a terrible storm.

Heaped and mounded in spontaneous bursts, glorious colorful flowers pocked the narrow track. Wild bouquets grew from spots where bodies had been dumped. Well-known to both local and national law enforcement agencies, Louisiana had no shortage of serial killers who used the wicked terrain as clandestine hunting and disposal grounds.

At the sight of the vivid blood-orange and golden marsh marigolds, a gracious warming relief overcame Remi as he stumbled out. He had found The Road of Flowers for the Dead, his escape. Whimpering in pain, he broke into a hobbled run along the backwater road.

Not ten yards in, sinister animals rushed from the woods. Ash-painted children were swathed in animal skins, fur covered their bodies, skinned livestock masks covered their small faces.

Hollowed pig-bone staffs, shaking and rattling, barred the way.

Howling in fear, Remi returned the way he came.

Chanting to the beating rhythms of ritualistic raja drums, The Creole Voodoo High Priestess stepped through the ghostly horde, taking the lead.

"Hail, Lord of the Bayou!" she commanded.

Her eyes were broken yolks of black ink pooling inside cutout holes of a horrid goat mask. Albino gator and patchwork snakeskins wrapped her lithe body.

Wiry goat fur lined her chin.

"Voodoo Maman?" A wimpling of recollection from what Levy had mentioned. "I'm a Thibodeaux." Remi's voice shook. "Born here. Like you. Our families have no beef."

The feeble attempt to negotiate fell flat, and the bone staff veered near his face, stumbling him back. Raja drums thundered in his ears, taut skins communing with ancestral Creole spirits.

Rushing blood hammered against his temples.

"Hail, Lord of the Swamp!" The Voodoo Priestess screamed like a wild banshee.

Rattling bones struck him on the chest.

He lurched sideways. A burning, biting, unholy pain from the jostling of his battered body erupted in a wail.

Remi turned and ran from the scary horde into the swampland.

"Hail, Lord of Dead Water Swamp!"

Incessant, nightmarish chants surged after him.

Waders stood mere inches from the water's edge. Late afternoon swirled in a sinister swill of murk and mist. Raja drums slowed to a languid, melancholic funeral procession.

Before him, The Priestess gripped a diamondback snake by its throat.

Hands of the fiendish children shuddered, then stilled.

"Hail, Parlangua." She spoke with grave reverence.

Then violently jammed the butt of her staff into the mud—a conjuring.

Cold dread pinched Remi's hyoid bone, the bone naturally broken when strangled to death. Water sluiced from sooty backs, cascading down in sheets as Parlangua answered the call.

Risen up on human hindlegs, they strode from black

waters. Reptilian paws squelched mud. Talons dragged. They circled, drenching him in nauseating vapors.

The Priestess lifted the snake, its body coiled tightly around her wrist.

Hissing Parlangua closed in.

A bizarre sense of familiarity struck him in the *Cocodrie* eyeshine. The largest, the acrobatic flipper from the boat, eclipsed Remi like a primeval god. An illusion of a face, sweet and kind and tender, superimposed its terrible head. Fingers traced an old polaroid until the technicolor wore off, memorizing every line and detail, long brushing strokes along lush blonde hair. Dismayed and distraught, Remi mashed his cheeks together between his frigid hands.

It wasn't possible.

"Maman?" he asked incredulously, pulling and plying his facial skin into various configurations, trying to reshape the malleable substance into something else.

They would lock him away in the psych ward forever.

"Is that really you?" Remi rambled. "But you died in childbirth. How can this be?"

Rumblings akin to guttural purrs puffed the terrible creature's scaly throat.

Remi twisted his body toward the abomination with frizzy black hair, scrutinizing the cold reptilian face in search of answers. Twirls of a coal-black moustache peeked beneath its slitted-nostrils, and his eyes widened, sclera shinny with a dismal understanding.

Thunderstruck, Remi recoiled. "Papa?!" he demanded. "You went out for a pack of Merlbot and never came back when I was only seven." His pointed finger shook accusingly. "Abandoned me like a sack of steaming shit."

"*Mais non, mon cher*, you must understand the way of

it." The Parlangua shaped sounds from regurgitated air flow, ticking its prehistoric head. "For us there is only the calling. A part of our DNA, years ago, a *Cocodrie* did an unspeakable act to a Thibodeaux woman, and we are the offspring of that unholy union, a legacy of things much more powerful than this world."

Which meant ...

The third ... was ...

Betrayal stung and broke him. Remi shook his head, sobbing. "No, not you too. How could you!" Disregarding the brutal mouth, he reached over it and tore a wad of algae growing from its scutes, Papaw's flattened gray tufts beneath. "Is this why you didn't fight back?"

"Does one lift a striking hand against God?" the monstrous voice creaked.

"Come." Their collective growls sizzled like water drops in smoking grease.

"Do what you must." The Priestess chewed through the agitated snake's neck, held its head in her mouth, decapitated body thrashing, unaware it was already dead.

Blood trickled through the wiry beard.

She spit out the serpent's head.

At the gruesome beheading, vile enlightenment triggered.

Chicken-necking for crabs.

A corpse served as bait, luring Remi back to the primordial soup of terrible origins.

Cocodrie eyeshine shone like guiding torchlights. Hypnotic whirls led him into turbid waters, through the parting pathway of radiant Chinese lanterns.

The Priestess hailed, heathen ghost children dancing all around, shrieking with abandon. Pig bones outpaced the heart-pounding blows of raja drums.

Sandwiched between three hideous hides, they took him deep. Rolling and rolling in their loving embrace, languid waves rocked him. A final image formed.

Bebe Etienne happily bouncing upon Zelda's knee. His son.

One day, Etienne would join them.

Humanity, shrinking and shriveling, Remi's plump human brain turned into a desiccated peach pit, programmed to kill, to survive, and ultimately to protect the sacred territory at any cost. In the darkling of savage change, his human body burst at the seams like an overstuffed meat casing, oozing out, the ooze boiled by a dead water broth, reconstituted into appalling gator parts, the original flavor preserved in its arms and legs, true to the syncretic spirit.

"Hail, Parlangua!"

Theo's words curled in a wisp of dissipating smoke. *What the swamp takes, it doesn't give back.* Somewhere deep in the murk, Great Lwizyàn's gilded fiddlesticks began to tap.

A zinging provocative jaunt was heard by ears attuned to the bayou's secret heartbeat.

The Bayou Butcher

James Kaine

"Celeste!" Thomas Boudreaux shouted as he dropped his coffee mug on the rickety wood porch, the ceramic shattering on impact. He nearly lost his balance as he missed a step while rushing toward the approaching figure.

It was just after 6:30 a.m., and Thomas had been on his way to Remy Motors, where he worked as a mechanic. It was a day like any other during the past six months—an anesthetized slog through the motions of pretending to be human, of trying not to act like he wasn't trapped in limbo between waning hope and creeping dread.

Exactly 180 days ago, his sixteen-year-old daughter, Celeste, had vanished, along with her best friend, Marie Goodwin, at whose house she was spending the night. Nothing in Marie's room appeared out of the ordinary, and there was no evidence of an abduction. They had vanished without a trace.

Police were called, flyers were posted, and search parties were dispatched into the bayou surrounding the small town of Beaux Marais. Despite weeks of exhaustive effort, neither the teenagers nor any evidence of their fate turned up. Thomas sobbed for the first time since he was a child when they called off the search.

Every day since was like living a waking nightmare. He and Marguerite barely spoke, opting to eat dinner in front of the television rather than suffering through silence at the dining room table with an empty chair between them. In his lowest moments, he cursed himself for preferring to learn his little girl was dead rather than living the rest of his life not knowing what had happened to her.

But when he saw the frail figure stumble into view through the morning mist, he got his answer. His daughter was alive. And she was coming home.

Thomas felt the crunch of the gravel driveway give way to the firmer asphalt as he bounded into the street.

"Oh my god! Celeste!" Marguerite's voice echoed from behind, her lighter footsteps joining her husband's.

The girl did not adjust her pace to meet her parents, but Thomas closed ground quickly, his wife on his heels. He threw his arms around his daughter, but she didn't return the embrace, her arms dangling limply at her sides. Marguerite joined in the hug but, like Thomas, quickly understood that, yes, their daughter was home.

But she was not okay.

Celeste spent three days in the hospital. She was dehydrated and malnourished but otherwise unharmed. To her parents' immense relief, there was no evidence of assault, physical or sexual. Still, questions remained. Where had she been for the past six months? And where was Marie?

The latter inquiry was the most pressing, especially to the police and to Marie's father, Jameis.

As soon as Celeste was well enough, the questions began, but her answers were vague. She presented confusion, having trouble with specifics at first. But through the gentle persistence of lead investigator Detective Evangeline Guidry, some answers emerged.

On the night they disappeared, Celeste had been sleeping at Marie's house. They went to bed around midnight, but Celeste recalled waking around three a.m. to find Marie gone. She went to the window and saw her friend heading toward the trees. The Goodwin house sat on the edge of the bayou, making wandering off at night particularly dangerous.

Confused and concerned, Celeste left the house to chase after Marie. She caught up with her quickly but said she looked to be in a daze. Celeste snapped her out of it, but they soon found they were lost, unable to find a path back to the house.

The teens spent an entire day trying to find their way back. Finally, they passed out under a tree from exhaustion. When Celeste came to, she found herself bound and gagged while being dragged through the woods by a large man.

Thomas almost didn't want to know, but he and Marguerite urged her to tell Detective Guidry what happened after that. She insisted she couldn't recall. All she remembered was that the man had taken them to a small house on stilts deep in the bayou.

"How did you escape?" the detective asked.

"I don't know," Celeste answered robotically. "All I remember is Dad running up and hugging me in the street."

"What about the man?" Guidry asked. "Do you remember what he looked like?"

"He was big," Celeste replied in the same mechanical tone. "Like one of those WWE guys. He had long black hair that covered his face and a big snake tattoo that wrapped around his whole left arm."

Guidry's jaw tightened. Thomas and Marguerite exchanged a knowing glance.

"Are you sure?" the detective asked.

Celeste nodded as her eyes glazed over. Within moments, she was asleep.

Guidry tilted her head toward the door, ushering the Boudreauxes out into the hall.

"It couldn't be ..." Marguerite started when they were out of the room, trailing off as she understood she couldn't support the assertion.

"He was never captured," Guidry countered the unfinished claim.

"But he stopped over thirty years ago," Thomas said.

"As far as we know," Guidry qualified.

The *He* they spoke of was the infamous Bayou Butcher, a serial killer who terrorized Beaux Marais and the surrounding area since the early 1970s. The Butcher would start a killing spree that would last several months at a time before abruptly stopping for long stretches ranging from six months to nearly three years. But after his last rampage in 1994, he disappeared, seemingly for good. As years turned to decades, the madman was relegated to just another bayou legend, like the

Rougarou or the voodoo Loas.

The case frustrated every detective who took it on. If it wasn't for the similarities in the victims—all grotesquely mutilated, with a crude snake symbol carved into what little flesh remained—there would be nothing linking them to the same killer. He left no other physical evidence. His only misstep was getting caught on a trail camera in 1992 while dragging Annabelle Marsh into the swamp. The footage wasn't ideal, but it would have been good enough for identification if his face hadn't been obscured by long tangles of dark hair.

Still, his size and the distinctive snake tattoo wrapping around the entirety of his left arm provided some identifiable features.

But thirty-one years was more than ten times longer than the killer's next longest hiatus. The police didn't know how old he would be, but he had to be close to sixty at best. The description Celeste gave, sparse as it may have been, painted an image of a person in their physical prime.

Age aside, a man living in the bayou for that long would need to stay in good shape. And the description of the house was the first real lead they had since the nineties, when Guidry's uncle worked the case.

"So what now?" Thomas asked.

"We go find that house."

"No. Absolutely not," Thomas said emphatically.

"I understand what I'm asking," Guidry acknowledged, "but we're out of options."

"There has to be another way," Marguerite added.

"You can't take her back out there!"

"Easy for you to say!" Jameis Goodwin blurted, drawing a frustrated brow furrow from the detective. "Your daughter is home safe! Mine is still out there in the hands of a maniac!" The man's voice, rich with a Haitian Creole accent, cracked at the end.

Thomas sympathized. Three weeks ago, it felt like his daughter was gone forever. But she was home, and even though she still faced a long road to mental recovery, she was alive. Celeste's return and revelation that Marie had survived sparked new hope in Jameis Goodwin. His wife had run out on them when Marie was a toddler, leaving his daughter the only person he truly cared for.

Thomas couldn't imagine how hard it was to lose that renewed sense of hope.

After Celeste's questioning at the hospital, Guidry had mobilized units to search the bayou for the stilted home. But three weeks later, they had found nothing. Search parties scoured the area on foot, by boat, and even by helicopter. Search dogs and infrared scans failed to yield any clues. They were dangerously close to returning to square one.

Which was why Guidry and Jameis Goodwin showed up at the Boudreaux family's door, desperation hanging over the latter.

The detective proposed taking Celeste with them into the bayou for one last search. Even though she said she didn't remember how she escaped, let alone how she made it home, Guidry hoped taking her back would trigger something—anything—in her memory to help them find Marie.

"I wouldn't ask if we hadn't exhausted all other options," Guidry admitted.

Thomas looked at Jameis, his heart breaking for the

man. The two were little more than acquaintances because of their daughters' friendship, but he had gotten to know Marie well over the years. He wanted nothing more than to see her come home safely.

Unfortunately, Celeste being back gave Thomas the luxury of pragmatism. And with that came the macabre understanding that the more time passed, the less likely Marie would be found alive. He understood every raw emotion suffocating her father. But he couldn't risk his daughter's life—not to mention her already fragile sanity—by sending her back into the bayou.

Thomas opened his mouth, still searching for the words to deny the desperate man's request. He didn't find them, but he didn't need to as Celeste answered on her own behalf.

"I'll go."

All parties turned toward the stairs, startled as they were unaware the subject of their debate had joined them.

"Absolutely *not*!" Marguerite said, intercepting Thomas's chance to comment just as his daughter had seconds earlier.

"It's not your call, Mom," Celeste replied.

Her tone unsettled Thomas. Much of her limited dialogue since her return had a stilted, emotionless tone, but it particularly stood out at that moment. He had borne witness to countless mother-daughter verbal sparring sessions, each exuding a level of passion beyond whatever the trivial catalyst may have been. But the dispassionate way in which she countered her parent's assertion was disconcerting.

Marguerite must have felt the same because she didn't offer her typical pointed rejoinder. She instead fell into a befuddled silence, while Thomas's own response died on his tongue.

"I have to," Celeste added unprompted. "Marie needs me."

Guidry mobilized her team quickly. Despite Celeste's proclamation that she would join the search, Thomas was not going to allow her to go without him. The detective didn't object. Nor did she try to convince Jameis Goodwin not to come. Marguerite agreed to wait at home even though her anxiety was palpable, visibly trembling as she hugged her husband and daughter goodbye.

The team was rounded out with three additional members.

Freddy Brock was a sergeant with Beaux Marais PD. He was more than a head taller than Thomas's five foot eleven inches and had the physique of a tank. It was said that the Butcher was built like a pro wrestler, but Thomas couldn't imagine he was bigger than that guy.

Jorge Avalos was Brock's polar opposite. He was maybe an inch shorter than Thomas, with a lean physique. A BMPD patrolman, he was covered in tattoos on almost every visible patch of skin up to his neck. Some of the ink Thomas recognized as gang-related, knowledge he had from his own misspent youth. Officer Avalos had clearly switched paths somewhere along the way.

Finishing the crew was Kervens Moise. Unlike the others, he was not law enforcement, nor did he have any personal connection to the case. He was a local trapper, and according to Guidry, his knowledge of that area of the bayou was second to none.

But Kervens's lack of personal investment wasn't the only thing that stood out to Thomas. The cops were all business. If they were frightened at the prospect of venturing into the bayou to hunt a serial killer, they were trained well enough not to show it. Jameis was so determined to find his missing daughter he didn't have time for fear. Celeste remained eerily detached which, to Thomas, was as unnerving as the prospect of what might be waiting for them in the marsh. But Kervens was the only one other than himself who seemed nervous about what they were ready to do.

In fact, the man was downright skittish, fumbling with his pack as much as his words.

"This is not smart," he said to himself while tapping the glass on his pocket compass, his accent thicker than Jameis's. "No, this thing we about to do is not a good idea. Not at all."

"Put a lid on it, Moise," Brock ordered. "You're spooking the civilians."

"Civilians?" Kervens asked incredulously. "What you think I am, big boy?"

"A volunteer. *They've* got kids out here," Avalos interjected. "You got kids, Kervens? I do. So unless you know what these men are going through, I suggest you keep your mouth shut."

"Or you could just shut the fuck up for the sake of my ears," Brock added.

"Put a lid on it!" Guidry chastised.

Brock huffed and offered a half-hearted, "Sorry, boss."

"I'm just saying this ain't smart," Kervens continued. "Ain't none of us coming out if we go too far."

"And that's enough out of you," Guidry said, directing her ire to their guide. "You agreed to help. Either do it without commentary or go home."

Kervens paused and fiddled with his pack some more, finishing his prep and slinging it over his shoulders.

"Then help I will," he said with resignation. "Let's go."

A little over an hour had passed since the search party entered the bayou, and for the first time, Thomas was starting to think they might have been lost.

"Does any of this look familiar, Celeste?" Guidry asked. Thomas picked up on a slight change in her inflection that made him wonder if she thought the same.

"No," Celeste admitted matter-of-factly.

At first, Thomas's daughter had directed them confidently. But the farther they ventured, the less frequent her instructions became. They had been traversing the increasingly soggy terrain for over twenty minutes since the teen had last spoken.

Heightened tension thickened the already dense air, blanketing the group as their optimism waned. Everyone felt it, but it was Kervens who voiced it. "We be going too far," the skittish trapper said. "There be only bad things waiting where we headed."

"Worse than a demented serial killer?" Avalos asked acerbically, punctuating the query with a laugh. Kervens didn't share the cop's amusement.

"Is a hungry gator worse than a man with a knife? Maybe, maybe not. You end up dead either way. That gon' bring you comfort when the lights go out?"

"Hold up!" Thomas shouted, grabbing Kervens by the arm, creating a domino effect that stopped the party in its tracks. "Are you talking about gators, killers, or something else?"

Kervens's eyes bulged, and sweat beaded on his forehead. "You don't want to know," he said. "Believe you me.

"Bullshit!" Thomas snapped back. "My daughter is not going any further unless you tell us what we're up against!"

"Calm down, Mr. Boudreaux," Guidry said, stepping in between the men. "This isn't helping."

"What isn't helping is Mr. Moise here!" Thomas exclaimed. "He's supposed to be our guide, but all he's done is tell us we shouldn't be here. Why are you even with us? Do you even know where we are?"

"Dad ..." Celeste's voice was low, and the argument continued as if they didn't hear her.

"It's *because* I know this bayou that I'm telling you this. We need to go back ... before it's too late," Kervens said, his tone adamant.

"Dad ..."

"We can't go back!" Jameis blurted. "Marie is still out there!"

"I'm sorry, but I can't put Celeste in danger again. I just can't."

"Dad!"

Celeste got their attention that time, her raised voice startling the others in the first genuine display of emotion since she had come home. Everyone fell silent and turned their attention to the teenager as she slowly raised her hand, pointing behind them.

The party turned back to see what she wanted them to see. When he saw it, Thomas's bones iced over.

A clearing had opened in the trees. Not that they had missed it—it had *not* been there. The path they were traversing was narrow, with no outlet in sight. But there was a gap as wide as a house leading to a big open area with a large pond in the center.

The heavy silence that fell over the group told Thomas that they were as shocked as he was.

"Where the fuck did that come from?" Brock asked, giving voice to what everyone was thinking.

"I told you!" Kervens exclaimed. "I told you there be bad things in this bayou!"

"Stop talking in riddles, goddamn it!" Jameis shouted, desperation wearing his patience. "What the hell is going on?"

It was Celeste who answered, her arm still outstretched. "The house. It was there."

"Was?" Guidry asked.

"Off to the right," Celeste answered. "It was there." She lowered her finger. "It was there, but now it's not."

"How the fuck is that possible?" Avalos asked.

"I told you!" Kervens yelled. "I told you!"

"Quiet!" Guidry commanded. The commotion settled enough for her to ask Celeste, "Are you sure this is the spot?"

"Yes," the girl replied. "The house was there!"

More questions raced through Thomas's head, but he didn't ask them. It was clear they were in a situation they couldn't explain. Even worse, they were unprepared.

The sky above them darkened. Thomas looked at his watch. It was three p.m. It was too early for sunset, and there were no storms in the forecast. The rest of the group noticed too, tension again suffocating the surrounding air.

"We're heading back," Guidry announced. "Right now."

"We can't!" Jameis cried. "Marie!" He tried to push

forward, but Brock and Avalos restrained him. "Get your fucking hands off me!" he demanded in vain.

"Calm down, Mr. Goodwin," Brock said.

The manic father stopped struggling, but his demeanor was anything but *calm*.

Guidry locked eyes with him. "I understand, Mr. Goodwin," she said calmly but insistently. "But we're losing daylight. We're not giving up. We're just regrouping."

Jameis fell still and quiet. Tears welled in his eyes. Thomas's priority was Celeste, but his heart went out to the man. If the roles were reversed? He would be just as desperate.

"We'll find her," Guidry assured.

Thomas didn't find that convincing.

"This is fucking insane!" Brock blurted.

Thomas shared the sentiment. He checked his watch and saw it was just after seven p.m. They had been trying to get back to their base camp for over four hours, but each time they thought they were on the right path, it would lead them somewhere unfamiliar. They weren't just lost. They were trapped.

"This shit ain't possible," Avalos added as he pulled a small gold cross from under his shirt and kissed it. "It just ain't!"

"I warned you!" Kervens said. "We be in it now!"

No one gave the trapper any shit that time. He had been right about that part of the bayou. The environment was unnatural.

At that time of year, the sun would typically be

setting, but it was dark as midnight. At no point could they see the moon through gnarled tree branches that had been lush with greenery hours earlier but at that moment looked dead and even burned. If not for their flashlights, they wouldn't have been able to see in front of themselves.

"This is like before," Celeste said, her tone flat and analytical. "This is what happened to me and Marie."

"What does that mean?" Jameis asked.

"It means he's coming."

The group had picked up their pace but had still failed to find their way out. Almost six hours had passed since the clearing had opened to the empty spot where Celeste claimed the Butcher's house had been. The darkness intensified, and the tactical flashlights struggled to pierce it. Even worse, the bayou typically cooled once the sun went down, but that wasn't the case then. A suffocating heat thickened the air, weighing down the group's lungs and making traversing the unsteady ground even more difficult.

Thomas felt the effects. His shirt clung to his skin, and he felt the sweat from his feet pooling in his boots. His lungs felt like twin anvils in his chest; he had to force himself to take slow, deliberate breaths as each exhalation stung as if lined with razor wire.

He kept a cautious eye on Celeste. If the trek was as taxing on his daughter as it was on him, she wasn't showing it. Her skin was slicked with sweat, the same as the others, but she moved steadily and her breathing remained even.

What happened to her out here? Thomas lamented.

There was so much of his little girl walking next to him—her face, her voice, some of her mannerisms—but it also felt as if so much was missing. They needed to get her into therapy when they got out of the bayou.

IF we get out of the bayou.

"Stop!" Kervens shouted without warning, his distinctive accent pulling Thomas from his thoughts.

The party stopped moving, and flashlight beams danced in the darkness as its members instinctively searched for what had startled the man.

"What is it?" Guidry asked.

Kervens was looking around, almost as if he didn't hear the detective, but he answered. "There's something ... different."

"No fucking shit," Avalos said.

Guidry ignored him, keeping her focus on the trapper. "What do you mean, dif—"

Her follow-up was interrupted by an ear-splitting scream. The crew trained their lights on the source, illuminating her as if she was the star of some macabre stage show.

Thomas grabbed Celeste's shoulders as she continued to wail. He felt the tremors quake her body, uncontrollable even in his firm grip. He cried, "Stop!"

"Celeste!"

"What the fuck is wrong with her?" Brock exclaimed.

"Sweetheart, please! What's wrong?"

As abruptly as the episode began, it stopped without warning. The girl fell statue-still and dead quiet. Thomas released her shoulders and took a step back as the shaky flashlight beams continued lighting her.

After several tense moments, she spoke. "He's here."

The words triggered chaos. As soon as they left her

lips, every flashlight beam went out simultaneously. Thomas reached to pull Celeste in close but grabbed at air. A cacophony of shouts, grunts, and curses emanated from the surrounding darkness.

That was just the start.

Celeste screamed again. That was followed by a sound that reminded Thomas of a knife being pulled from a block. Thomas's blood ran cold as that was accompanied by a squelching sound, followed by a man's pained grunt. Before he could register what had happened, loud cracks sounded as muzzle flares temporarily flashed through the darkness. Another man, sounding like Avalos, screamed.

Thomas lunged forward toward his daughter's cries, hoping to reach her as he dropped to the ground, but came up empty, crashing into the sodden grass.

"Hold your fire, goddamn—"

It was Guidry who issued the command, but she was cut off before finishing it. More obscene squelches and anguished cries echoed through the night before it again fell silent.

Thomas knew moving could put him in danger, but he had to find Celeste. As he braced himself to push off the ground, he saw lights glow as the downed flashlights somehow regained their function.

Thomas scrambled to the nearest one, retrieving it and frantically waving the beam in search of his daughter. The light revealed an abattoir instead.

Brock's large frame rested against a tree. The man's sizable body would have been necessary to identify him, as his head was no longer attached. Or it would have been necessary if the cop's head wasn't lying in his lap. Thomas let the light linger on the ghastly sight longer than he should have out of sheer frozen terror. When a rogue spurt of blood erupted from the stump of the dead man's neck, splashing on his forehead, Thomas finally moved the light away.

It was only a few feet, which was all it took to find Avalos.

The smaller man was broken, every limb twisted at unnatural angles. His vest had been pulled up, allowing his killer space to rip open Avalos's stomach. A rope of intestine had been pulled from the cavity and wrapped twice around the man's neck. His face was purple, and his bloodshot eyes looked as if they were on the verge of falling out of their sockets.

Panic erupted inside Thomas as he turned 180 degrees.

"Celeste! Where are you?"

"Thomas!"

The reply was from Jameis. Thomas pointed the beam toward the sound of the man's voice. He found him quickly, but the beam also revealed a third corpse.

Guidry.

The lead detective was not mutilated as her compatriots were. A hole almost directly dead center on her forehead still smoked from the bullet that ended her life. A growing puddle of blood underneath told them it had gone completely through.

"Christ!" Jameis shouted.

"Celeste!" Thomas bellowed again. And again, it was someone else who answered.

"Here!" Kervens announced in a shaky voice.

Thomas trained the light on him. A second beam soon followed as Jameis had retrieved another flashlight.

Relief flooded Thomas when he saw the trapper leading Celeste out from behind a tree. He rushed over to embrace his daughter. Yet again she didn't return it, but there was no time to worry about that.

"We have to get the hell out of here!" Kervens said in the understatement of the century.

Jameis picked up Guidry's pistol. Thomas looked back at the dead policemen on the other side. Both were armed with automatic rifles, but Thomas didn't want to take them. Putting aside that he had no experience handling that type of gun, one of them had probably fired the shot that killed Guidry. He didn't want his fingerprints on it. They would have enough problems, assuming they survived.

Instead, he pulled Avalos's Glock from its holster.

"Follow me!" Kervens ordered.

"How is that there?"

Jameis said what Thomas was thinking. They had been running for the past twenty minutes, following Kervens, who continued to lead Celeste by the hand toward what they hoped was a way out.

But somehow they had come to the clearing again. At least they thought it was. The difference was that a dilapidated house stood where Celeste had initially claimed it was.

How was that possible?

"Is that it?" Jameis asked, hope and dread mingling in his words.

Yes," Celeste confirmed.

That was all the desperate father needed to hear. He broke into a sprint straight to the ominous structure, caution be damned.

"Wait!" Thomas shouted after him.

"Damn fool is going to get hisself killed!" Kervens observed.

Thomas wanted to go after him, to try to save the man from himself. There was also a morbid desire to know what was inside. It was no doubt a place of unfathomable evil; if he knew what his daughter faced in there, maybe he could help her.

But it was the part of him that couldn't imagine harm befalling his child that won out. He did not want to know.

Celeste took the decision out of his hands.

Like Jameis, she took off running, faster than Thomas had ever seen her move.

"Celeste!" he called to her.

The girl ignored him as she ran to the killer's lair.

Thomas was twenty yards behind his daughter when she took the rickety back stairs two at a time. The girl had practically been a zombie since her return, yet she had somehow become a world-class sprinter.

A moment before she disappeared inside, he heard Jameis scream from somewhere within. It was a horrid, inhuman sound he would not have thought the man capable of.

Ten seconds later, he understood why.

He burst through the door. His first response was relief as Celeste stood just inside the entrance, unharmed. But over her shoulder, a gruesome scene revealed itself.

Jameis Goodwin sat on the floor cradling the ruined corpse of his daughter.

She looked as if she had been dead for months. Thomas didn't need to be a medical expert to know the body showed signs of mummification. Beyond that, the killer had certainly lived up to his moniker.

She was *butchered*.

Her hands and feet were severed, as was her left leg to halfway up her thigh, a darkened, jagged piece of bone jutting out of the stump.

Her shirt was torn open, and she was sliced from gut to gullet. Like Avalos, her innards were hanging out of the cavity. But they were rotted and withered. Her throat was slit, a crimson crust staining everything underneath. Two hollow sockets sat where her eyes once were, and a crude etching of a snake was carved starting from her forehead, over the spot where her nose used to be, finally coming to a stop at her chin.

Her father rocked the lifeless husk as he continued to wail.

Thomas grabbed Celeste and turned her toward him. The girl didn't resist, but she didn't show emotion, either. The urgency she displayed in taking off was completely gone.

As he held his daughter, powerless to help the devastated man before him, he caught sight of another corpse. It was back toward the opposite end of the room.

It was a man, a big one. Like Marie, it seemed he had been dead for months. His stained undershirt and jeans hung off his withered frame. Strands of dark, stringy hair splayed out underneath his head, and a large snake tattoo was still barely visible, wrapped around the grayed skin of his left arm.

It was The Bayou Butcher.

The giant cleaver bisecting his face was very obviously the cause of death. Despite the grime and rot that blanketed every corner of the room, it somehow looked pristine, the metal glinting in the moonlight filtering through the cracks in the wall.

None of it made sense. Marie looked as the Butcher's other victims had been described. She had been dead for a long time, but so had the Butcher. Yet, somehow Celeste had not only remained unharmed but had stayed there for months on her own.

Did she...?

Thomas didn't finish the thought as Jameis yelled, drawing his attention.

"You!" the grieving father shouted.

Thomas saw the man's murderous gaze directed at Celeste.

"You!" he repeated as he pointed Guidry's pistol at her.

There wasn't time for questions. Thomas could only react. He raised Avalos's gun and pulled the trigger without thinking. The first bullet ripped through Jameis's throat, a jet of blood spattering Marie's desecrated corpse.

Jameis was staggered but lifted the weapon again. Thomas pulled his own trigger again and again, dropping the man in a frantic hail of bullets.

As the hollow click confirmed the gun was empty, he heard a voice with a familiar accent behind him.

"I think you got him, man."

Thomas whirled and saw Kervens standing in the doorway. Only it wasn't.

The trapper's face appeared to be covered in white greasepaint, resembling a skull. Gone was the jumpsuit he wore for the search, replaced with a black suit and an orange vest, the tails of his coat hanging down past his knees. A top hat rounded out the look, the brim adorned with tiny skulls and feathers matching the vest.

However, the most jarring thing about the man's transformation was the giant cobra draped over his shoulders like a leathery, venomous scarf.

"You …" Thomas said, unintentionally mimicking the man he had just shot dead. "You … you're …"

"Spit it out, Tommy boy," *Kervens* said as he lit a cigar, the musty smoke mingling with the fetid slaughterhouse stench. "You know who I be."

"Baron Samedi," Thomas said almost reverently.

"Give the man a cigar!" The Baron shouted with glee. "I have extras if you'd like one."

Thomas couldn't believe it. Standing in front of him was the Loa of the Dead, a being that everyone in Beaux Marais had heard of but, until that moment, Thomas did not think truly existed.

"What … what's happening?" Thomas asked, feeling as if he was drunk.

"What's happening is that you totally fucked that motherfucker up! Shit, man, you turned him into a big ole block of Swiss cheese!"

"Why?"

Samedi looked confused. "Because he was going to fucking shoot you! I'd have done the same damn thing."

"No," Thomas said weakly. "Why … this? Why … the Butcher?"

"Oh, that asshole?" Samedi said. "He was a fan. Was always leaving me rum and cigars and shit. Excellent stuff too, not that mass-produced Bacardi bullshit."

"He killed for you?"

"What are you, fucking high? I don't make people kill for me. You dipshit humans do that just fine on your own."

"I don't understand."

"Oh, for fuck's sake, Tommy, stay with me here. Butcher here kept dying. Fucking heart attack in the '70s, cancer in the '80s. The dumb fuck even got poisoned by a snake in '91. But he knew how to appeal to my more benevolent nature, so I kept resurrecting him until he finally got on my nerves."

"What do you—"

Thomas didn't get to finish his question as he felt a sudden sharp pain in the back of his head. His vision blurred, and he lost his balance, falling to his knees.

"I told him he needed to chill the fuck out," Samedi continued as if nothing had happened. "But he wouldn't listen. So, 'bout thirty years back, I told him no more. You think he would have gotten the hint, but he was one dense motherfucker."

Thomas's thoughts were muddled. He couldn't register everything that was happening, but he saw Celeste step around him and stand next to the Baron. In her hand was the cleaver, dripping with fresh blood. With Thomas's blood.

"He invoked Marinette. How this motherfucker knew so much about us is beyond me, but she is much less *friendly* than me. In fact, she's the most violent bitch you ever gonna meet. She fucking loves killing."

Thomas tried to open his mouth, to appeal to his daughter one last time, but he didn't see her. He saw a woman he didn't recognize. It wore Celeste's face, but the evil grin stretched across it was something else. Something inhuman.

He fell over onto his side. Darkness closed in.

"Marinette entertained the big dumb fuck for decades. He would bring folks here—well, when the bayou allowed them in, that is—and torture and kill them for Mari's pleasure. She never took much interest in any of them. But I guess she really liked your daughter."

"She was just so ... pure," the thing in Celeste's body said. "Corrupting the innocent is so fucking satisfying! That was enough to get me off of the sidelines." She looked down at the hands of the teen she possessed. "You did a good job raising her. And I'm going to have fun with this one for a long, long time."

The Loa leaned down and kissed Thomas on the cheek. In that last moment, she sounded like Celeste again.

"Goodnight, Daddy."

The sun was rising over the town of Beaux Marais as the thing that looked like Celeste Boudreaux walked down the street toward Celeste's house, cleaver in hand. She would pay the girl's mother a visit first. She had lost everything, anyway. Killing her would be a mercy. After that, the world was her oyster.

The Bayou Butcher would hunt again.

Screams from the Bayou

Heather Ann Larson

Graves will rumble,
The earth will shake.
The water will boil
And bones will break.

Sabine mixed the bones in her hand and tossed them onto the make-shift table in front of her. The candlelight inside the shack was dim, and the blackened sky outside further darkened the shadowed room. The rain was torrential, the thunder a deafening drum, the lightning immediately outside her door giving the room a glaring brightness when it struck. Her mood had a tendency to influence the weather, and that fantastic display of power from the gods was no exception.

That charlatan, Téofil Leblanc, had dipped his toes

into places they didn't belong, in waters that weren't his to wade in. His britches done got too big, and he thought he could sling her name through the mud, sully her reputation with his cheap parlor tricks.

She would make sure her name never slithered off his tongue again. *It will be hard to utter* any *name with no tongue*, she thought. A smile that would terrify even a monster graced her face.

Her serpent-like tongue flicked out, tasting the air. She tasted a whiff of deceit and fear and knew he was close to breaking. Her grin grew, breaking her face into something that looked like two halves stacked together to make a whole. Nobody had ever messed with the voodoo priestess and lived to tell the tale. She would inflict pain upon Téofil that he could never in his wildest dreams have imagined.

Her Rougarou, Sazerac, lay at her feet, a low growl vibrating her foot where his head lay upon it. In the history of priestesses, Sabine was the only one to ever conquer a Rougarou and keep it for herself. With the appearance of a werewolf, but with light gray fur and twice as big both in height and musculature, his presence was intimidating to all but her. His loyalty was unfailing; he had been by her side for 125 years. He would retrieve the swindler for her—his nose had never let her down.

She knocked back her drink, named the same as her Rougarou, and gathered her bones. She placed them back into their deep-purple velvet bag and pulled the drawstring tight. Putting them in her leather hip satchel, she stood, closed her eyes, and inhaled a deep breath, filling her lungs as much as possible before slowly releasing her air.

Suddenly, her eyes flew open. Instead of their normal

chocolate color, they were crimson. Her nostrils flared, and a guttural moan escaped her lips. He was close, and he had hell to pay. His bill had come due.

Starting as a pickpocket at an early age, six years old to be exact, Téofil had always been a little shit, a trickster, a liar. He grew up on the streets of New Orleans, filching what he could to get by. His father had abandoned the family three years previous, and his mother spent her every waking hour working to scrape enough money by to put some measly cabbage soup on the table. So Téo did what he could to help. And while his mother hated liars and thieves, never did she turn down the offerings he gave her at the end of the day. With six mouths to feed, she had to do what she had to do; she simply didn't ask questions.

Thirty years later, he knew there were areas of New Orleans he should not have been gracing, particular those areas close to the graveyard and the area around Sabine's joint. And mostly he stayed away from those places. But they were prime pickings and sometimes he just couldn't help himself. He was always more aware of his surroundings on those days, keeping a keen eye to the shadows and back alleys, making sure her loyal subjects weren't watching him.

That day was going to be the day that changed his life; he could feel it in the air. Everything felt electric, the air crackling around him as he strolled down Royal Street. He felt alive, wired, and the tune he whistled reflected his energy. He had a pep in his heeled Santonis, and his arms swung lightly at his sides. He was looking forward to what the day would bring.

He took up residence just inside the mouth of his usual alleyway and surveyed the scene. It was the end of June and heating up quickly, but the tourists were out in droves. The weather report called for mid-afternoon storms, so he knew the out-of-towners would be looking for their souvenirs early, wanting to get all their shopping in before the rain hit.

He also knew the tourists liked to say they played with a little magic or voodoo. He could help them with that. He knew they enjoyed the supposed dangers of messing with a bit of alleged black magic, finding their way down a darkened alley or maybe inside a cemetery and seeing a trick or hearing the future for a pretty penny. They did it just to say they did, to impress their coworkers and best friends when they returned to their posh homes and their lazy lives. All they got from him was a cheap trinket, bought in bulk, and a blank stare from the small bit of glamour he was actually able to perform. They also found their wallets empty the next time they reached for them. Téo never felt guilty taking money from those uptight, rich assholes who thought they were dabbling in a little dangerous fun.

Just as he took a half-step forward to filch a wallet sticking out of a woman's Louis Vuitton, a cold breeze kissed his neck and a shadow, invisible on the sidewalk, caressed his cheek. He withdrew his arm, shivers racking his body. The shadow continued its stroking, running itself down the side of his neck and across his collar bone even though his shirt was buttoned all the way.

When he thought he wouldn't be able to take the shaking any longer, the shadow retracted and he stopped trembling. *Mama woulda said a goose walked over my grave*, he thought. *What in the world was that?* The shadow was gone, and so was Téofil's confidence. He needed to get out of there, get home. He knew what that was. He knew he had been playing with fire in Sabine's joint, stealing from her customers right under her nose. How could he ever have thought he would get away with that?

Word on the street was Sabine was the strongest voodoo priestess in history—even stronger than Marie Leveau. She was a strong healer, an even stronger prognosticator, and a woman known to dole out punishment if you interfered with her. She owned the establishment anybody practicing the old religion went to. Everybody knew there were regular poker games there, and the customers tended to have heavy pockets.

Téo liked to help lighten their load. He had been certain he kept himself hidden at the time, but reflecting back on what he did, he knew he had been foolish thinking he would get away with picking pockets in her place. *What the hell was I thinkin'?* he wondered. He had gotten a bit greedy and took too much, got sloppy.

He knew Sabine sent that shadow. The cold darkness across his face was gone, but the coldness in his chest lay heavy. His arm ached, and the pressure in his rib cage was enough to send him to his knees. It felt like something was squeezing his heart. He could feel the lub-dub of it off-kilter, stuttering. He took a few deep breaths (or as deep as he could with the heaviness in his chest making it feel like he couldn't expand his lungs enough) and blew them out slowly, closing his eyes and concentrating on making the rhythm right again.

He finally felt the grip of the priestess release his heart and the pace go back to its normal beat. He took several minutes to regain his composure, then wiped his brow with the lace-trimmed handkerchief in his breast pocket and stood. Using an abandoned crate to help steady himself, he held on until he felt he wouldn't topple over. Then he took a final deep breath, regained his confident composure, and headed straight for home. There would be no more pickpocketing that day, no parlor tricks to swindle the tourists. He needed to get low and stay down.

The heat of the day dissipated without warning, and low clouds moved in. The wind picked up something fierce, swirling debris from the street high into the air. Pedestrians sprinted for the closest open doorway or shop they could find to hide from the abrupt storm.

Téofil had stepped into another alleyway in an attempt to get out of the wind, but it followed him. Gravel and broken bottle glass picked up by the gales slammed into him, causing him to curl into the fetal position to make himself as small as possible.

A voice carried on the wind, a susurrus of a woman's chant brushing against his ear. *Graves will rumble; the earth will shake. The water will boil, and bones will break.* Sabine's hex danced through his brain, sending fear to the very core of his soul.

He cried out, "I beg yo forgiveness, yo highness. I know I done wrong, and I repent my transgressions. I beg you!" He lay there shaking and crying, his bruised and sliced body unable to handle the onslaught any longer.

The squall died as quickly as it started. People walked back into the street, looking at the sky, their faces displaying disbelief at what had happened and concern that it wasn't quite done. While the tourists would talk about the weird storm that happened upon them on their shopping excursion, the locals knew the truth.

Téofil pulled himself off the ground, brushed himself off, and sprinted home. He knew his mama would know what to do.

"Son, I done told ya to stop messin' with that hoodoo voodoo bullshit. Now look what you done got yo'self into. How you gonna make this one right, huh?" Stella Leblanc slapped her boy upside the head for the fourth time since he had come home. She knew he was playing parlor tricks on the street, and she knew eventually he would put himself in a bind he couldn't fight his way out of. How the hell was she supposed to help him with this one? Sabine was not a woman anybody messed with. Everybody knew that.

Sitting at the kitchen table in a fresh set of slacks and a dress shirt, his head hung so low his chin rested on his chest. His eyes were red rimmed, and his breath was still hitching. He wasn't built to run like he did, and the anxiety building in him was adding to his distress. Every time he thought of the darkness crawling across his skin, he shuddered and his heart rate skyrocketed. His wounds, cleaned and dressed by his dear, sweet mama, stung. And every time she whacked the back of his head, more tears poured down his face.

"I'll tell you what you gonna do, boy," Stella said. "You gonna go down to that house of sin and you gonna ask to talk to Miss Sabine directly. You gonna tell her you know ya done messed up and that ya are there to get on your knees and beg mercy. And you gonna tell her you'll work off yo penance however madam sees fit." There was no other way. Stella knew that unless her son confronted the woman and offered himself and his services, he was a dead man.

Téofil knew differently. "Mama, if I go walkin' in there, they gonna take me down right off the bat, no questions asked. Them body guards at the door knows who I am. Even if they didn't, Miss Sabine can smell a rat a hundred miles away, and that's what I am—a filthy rat." What he knew he had to do at that point was protect his mama, keep Sabine from going after the only woman Téo had ever truly loved.

New Orleans was small and the voodoo community even smaller; he heard all the stories of what happened to those who crossed Sabine. And he knew they were true, because he had seen some of those consequences firsthand. He considered that maybe his mama was right and that taking himself down there was the only way to keep his mama away from the priestess. But he was terrified of the consequences he may incur.

Waking in a cold sweat, Téofil knew sleep that night was done. The same dream had plagued him every night since the storm. Deciding to get up and shower the sticky stench off, he made his way to the bathroom in the dark, not turning any lights on so he didn't wake up his mama. The poor woman didn't sleep well as it was; she didn't need him making things worse.

Grabbing a fresh towel from the hall closet before he entered the bathroom, he paused. He heard a sound just before he closed the door. It sounded like the hiss and slither of the swamp snake Miss Sabine kept, Joshua.

Téo had never seen the thing before, but he had heard

stories. It was said that the snake was giant—thirty feet long and as thick as a man's thigh—and he didn't believe the stories to be false. That old man Walter down on Bayou Street told Téo all about that snake, claimed he was there when the thing came into Sabine's ownership. Téo had never known old man Walter to tell a fib in his life, so he knew it was the truth.

He shook, his body trembling all the way to its core. The thought of that thing in his mama's house, his mama sleeping just down the hall, put a terror into Téofil unlike anything he had ever previously experienced. It started in his legs and worked its way up, his abdomen tightening yet his bladder threatening to let go. His chest felt constricted, like the snake was already wrapped around him, crushing his ribs and taking away Téo's ability to breathe. His heart stuttered. His jaw chattered, his teeth clacking together like what he pictured Miss Sabine's bones to sound like when she threw them on the table during her predictions.

He turned his head first, then his body, all of his movements happening so painstakingly sluggishly it looked like a slow-mo video. He saw a shadow moving down the hall, through the kitchen. It was low to the ground and leisurely. And it came with that slinking sound of dry flesh against wood. It was Joshua; he hadn't been mistaken.

The next sound he heard caused his bladder to finally let go. A growl, guttural and malevolent, came from the back of the kitchen, near where the back door would have been. Téo knew he never should have gone to Sabine's joint, but he had no idea she knew the extent of what he had been up to. But clearly she did, because she sent Sazerac. It was at that point that Téo knew he was well and truly fucked. She never sent the Rougarou unless she meant to take life.

Confident though he was during his squandering and disillusionment of tourists that traveled to the area, deep down he was a coward. He was not a man of confrontation; he preferred to stay in the shadows, remain hidden from the eyes that mattered.

He had not done so. He had, in fact, done very much the opposite.

Although he was a weakling, he had a fierce love for his mama. He would not see her harmed for his misdoings. He steeled his resolve and took a few tentative steps toward the kitchen, planning to confront the two beasts. It was the last thing he wanted to do (and it might actually have been just that), but he needed to keep his mama safe.

His next step had him at the threshold. And he wasn't alone. A woman stood there, appearing within a blink. He inhaled to scream, but a fine powder was blown into his face and everything went dark.

He was floating through the void. There was no sound, no light, no color. There was only dark, and his fear. Yet the black was so pitch that even his fear couldn't take its true shape.

Then it was wet and malodorous. His surroundings smelled of damp rot and bog. The humidity was so thick it was hard to fill his lungs; it felt like he was breathing water. He felt himself tied down in a sitting position.

Opening his eyes, he saw he was exactly where he had guessed he would be.

Sabine's shack stood a short distance to his left.

A large bonfire burned in front of it, the wood still somewhat wet as it let off occasional snaps when the heat hit the moisture. Smoke poured out around the bottom of the fire, which Téo thought was odd that it stayed at ground level. The fire itself was the biggest blaze he had ever seen. It gave off an evil energy like it was there to consume.

He scanned the area around him, but it had to be near the witching hour because it was so dark he couldn't see much beyond the fire's reach. But he could hear something out there. Several somethings, in fact.

Sazerac's heavy breathing bristled the hair on Téofil's arms. The rasp of his phlegmy inhalations grated on Téo's ear drums. He could feel the Rougarou's heat against his back, smell the pungent odor pouring off the beast.

And he could hear Joshua's slow gyrations as he swam through the swamp. A snake was typically a quiet creature, coming upon a man with no warning. But Joshua wanted Téo to know he was there, so he made just enough rustling noise as he glided through the water to be noticeable.

A sharp claw grazed his cheek, running from the front of his face to the back, then drew a line down the back of his neck. Hot, reeking breath caressed his right ear, the stench causing him to gag. The breath switched to his other ear, along with what sounded like a purring growl. Sazerac was very happy, content, excited about what was going to happen.

Movement to his left. Sabine sauntered out of her shack, a simple dagger in her hand and a bone mask covering the top half of her face. Sashaying her way toward Téo, the glint in her eye said she had no plans to dispose of him quickly and quietly. There was a feral eagerness there that told him everything he needed to know.

"You have encroached on my territory for long enough, Téofil Leblanc. You have deceived people with your trinkets and cheap magic tricks for far too long. And you brought shame into MY house!" she thundered at him. Her voice echoed through the bayou, carrying across time and space. The depth of her accusation shook the water, causing ripples to lap up against Téo's strapped-down feet.

Joshua emerged from the water, rivulets of the bog cascading down his sleek skin. The way his body undulated across the ground, moving closer to Téo with painstaking slowness, taking his time with graceful purposefulness, ignited even greater fear in Téofil. The constrictor was smiling, if snakes could do such a thing. Joshua radiated excitement the closer he got to the man sitting in his swamp.

With Sazerac and Joshua ready to pounce upon Sabine's command, Téo couldn't take it anymore. He broke down sobbing, pleading for Sabine to either spare his life so he could change his ways or for her to end things quickly, to be done with it. The fear was crushing his chest; his heart was going too fast and it felt like it would explode. He couldn't catch his breath—the oxygen felt absent from the air, the thickness of the humidity not helping his hyperventilating. His body was shaking with such force he thought maybe it would simply give up the ghost and he would keel over dead as a doornail. He also thought maybe that would be better than what the voodoo priestess had in mind for him.

Sabine's laugh was deep, throaty, and cruel. There was no salvation or release in it; there was only pain and damnation. The darkness of her voice matched the pitch black of the swamp beyond the firelight.

She meandered up next to her Rougarou. In the thick humidity of the night, standing next to Sazerac's pale gray fur, her deep brown skin shimmered in the fire. The way the flames danced along the sheen of sweat across her collarbone was mesmerizing, drawing Téo's attention to the undulations there. He was hypnotized by her beauty; never before had he seen a woman so breathtaking that it hurt to look at her. His begging ceased, his eyes transfixed on hers.

So weak, this one, Sabine thought. *Hardly a glamour needed to dull his mind.* Sabine knew fear spoiled the meat, and she wanted the charlatan tasty for her pets. The meat would have been tainted enough when she finished with him. She also had no tolerance for the whimpering, whining, and begging he had displayed. *But what to do with him? Where do I start?*

The beasts picked up Sabine's thoughts. Sazerac's eyes gleamed brighter in the light of the fire, the orange reflection making them look like they were made of flame. He let out a quiet chortle, his teeth baring the smallest bit. Joshua hissed and grinned, flicking his tongue toward Téo, tasting the numb fear coursing through the man. The constrictor could tell the man was still afraid, but the glamour made it less, and that would be good for later eating.

Sabine traced a sharpened claw across Téo's chin, down his neck, and pierced his jugular—just a little, just for her pets to get a taste of the life they were so anxious to devour. She traced the flow down his neck, then licked her dagger-like nail. She was no cannibal, but blood fueled her power, heightened her senses, and sated her burning anger, diminishing it to a crackling ember.

The monsters lunged at Téo, and at the same time, Sabine let the glamour wane a bit. Téo whimpered, unable to do anything else, and tensed as the Rougarou lapped at his throat and as the snake wound its way around him, climbing his body, taking its time. The glamour loosened further, and Téo trembled. He was certain the wolf creature was going to rip out his throat. *That might be a blessing*, he thought. But as the snake's skin raked with the barest touch across his throat, Joshua's neck against his, Téo's shaking became violent, the chair almost tipping over.

An amused laugh escaped Sabine. "That is enough, my pets. You have had a sample of what you will get later. But now it is my turn." And before Téo could blink, thin lines began leaking blood along his face, raking from ear to ear across both cheeks and his forehead. She ran her razor-blade nails along his left arm next, sinking them deeper into his flesh than she did on his face. As her hand came away from his forearm, she drew a second blade from the sheath on her calf without notice and jammed it into his right leg.

The scream that came from Téofil echoed through the bayou. It wove its way between the grasses and trees, it landed on the ears of those that dwelled in the swamp. It sang to the dark entities living within the borders of Sabine's domain. It called them to her.

Graves will rumble,
The earth will shake.
The water will boil
And bones will break.

Sabine uttered the words, her inviting hex winding its way on the air through her territory. The water began to boil, and the ground shook as the hoards left their graves to come to her.

As the sound emanating from her captive further summoned her army, she went to her knees and removed Téo's toes in one slash of her dagger. She spun as she stood and went for his fingers on his right hand with her dagger. As each digit hit the ground, Joshua was there to gather them into his mouth, gulping them down whole.

"No more will you steal, Téofil Leblanc. No more will you swindle, lie, or cheat your way through my town and my club. You will lie in the dirt, bones broken, skin flayed, heart dead. You will suffer the pain of a thousand deaths and yet not die.

"And your mother will also pay your price."

The scream Téo unleashed ripped his throat. He tried to continue to scream as the masses of monsters descended upon him, breaking his bones and tearing at his flesh, but the blood flooding his lungs prevented the sounds from emerging. He was drowning in his own blood.

But he wasn't dying fast enough.

THE NEIGHBOR

ASHON RUFFINS

It had been a few weeks, and the Hoods hadn't quite settled in yet. That wasn't a surprise. Moving from Minnesota to a suburb near New Orleans would be a challenge for almost anyone. The intention was to get as far away as possible from the environment that had so many painful memories and start anew. A new job for Connie, a new school for Jacob, and a new home for both—a home not weighted with the stench of death.

The aroma saturating the evening air of the kitchen was enticing.

"Hey, Mama," Jacob said. He put his backpack on the kitchen counter.

"Hey, baby. How was school today?" Connie asked.

"It was fine. The kids are cool. I'm still getting used to their accents, though."

Connie laughed as she could relate to the struggles she had in the workplace as a carpetbagger.

"Well, from everything I've gathered from the people

who have lived here their entire lives, we're lucky. The cool weather came early this fall. I kinda have to agree with them; it's been real comfortable around here," Connie said.

Jacob smiled at the thought of it. "Definitely just as nice as Minnesota in the fall. October can get pretty comfortable and colorful from the fallen leaves. I like that part."

"I went for another float in the bayou today because it's been so comfortable. No one was around, and it was incredibly relaxing. It was perfect."

Jacob peered out the nearby window and watched as a familiar figure stood next to the bayou that was only a hundred feet from the backdoor of their home. The shirtless man stood next to the twisting body of the bayou while holding an enormous book. He had a powerful build and adorned alligator-skinned pants. A string of unidentified bones dangled from his wrist and neck. The man's eyes stared down at the oversized book as his lips mumbled in a repetitive manner.

Connie inhaled deeply. "Honey, our neighbor seems to be a nice man, but I want you to stay away from him. I don't know what the hell is going on, but I want you to keep your distance from Mr. Reginald. He's a bit of a weirdo, and although he's a sweet man, I've had my issues with him."

"That's not a problem. The guy creeps me out. He always stares at you with those big eyes, and he doesn't blink," Jacob said.

Jacob and Connie continued to peer out the bay window of their kitchen as the neighbor stood stiffened in front of the darkened waters of the bayou.

"I should have known there would be issues with this guy. It's only been a few weeks. I blew up one of the floating donut rafts and took a little relaxing night float after unboxing the kitchen, kinda like I did today. I was exhausted and dozed off a bit. It wasn't thirty minutes later that he came running out of his house, cursing at me, warning me about the dangers of the bayou," Connie said, her frustration apparent. "I paddled my way back to the edge and hopped out. That's when he rambled about hungry gators and their preference to feed at night. I could barely understand him with that thick Cajun accent."

"There are gators in the bayou?" Jacob's eyes widened as if he had just come down the stairs Christmas morning to a tree overcrowded with presents. "That's so cool! You think we'll see one in the backyard one day?"

"God, I hope not. Besides, you're only twelve years old. If you see one back there, I need you to stay as far away from it as you can. Do you understand me?" Connie's face was intentionally stern in a way that only a mother could convey.

"Yeah, yeah, I got it. How cool would it be to see one up close, though?"

"Not cool. It's dangerous." Connie sighed. "I'm done eating. I wasn't really that hungry, anyway. That freak show of a neighbor seems to have made his way back inside. Just the thought of the scars on his shirtless torso has ruined my appetite." Connie rushed from the table, clearing the dishes in the process. "If you've done your homework, the rest of the night is yours for gaming."

Jacob rose from the table with his brow curled as he glared at his mother. "Why are you in such a rush?" he asked.

Connie didn't bother to turn and face him. "I have an after-hours gathering with some coworkers. Gotta go out and make some friends and do some networking.

We're still new to the city, you know."

Jacob rolled his eyes, grabbed his handheld gaming device, and plopped down on the couch.   His eyes focused on the flashing lights on the screen. "I guess you gotta do what you gotta do," Jacob mumbled.

Connie's lip curled as she glared at Jacob's slouching shoulders and bratty attitude. It wasn't unusual for her twelve-year-old son not to want her to leave the house, especially at night.

"Baby, I'm not going out to find a replacement for your father. No one can replace him. But it's been six months since the accident. I just can't close myself off from everyone," Connie said.

"You promise, Mama?" Jacob asked, his eyes watering at the thought of his late father.

"I promise, baby." Connie smiled. "I'm going to get ready. I have to be at the restaurant in thirty minutes. It's Friday night, so you're free to stay up all night gaming if you want. Just keep the doors and windows locked, and don't answer the door for anyone. Do you understand?"

"I get it. Yes, I understand."

A few hours passed, and Jacob slept peacefully, the blaring sounds and flashing lights of his video game active as it lay upon him, until a loud crashing sound nearby jolted him from his rest. Jacob jumped out of his bed, and his handheld gaming system crashed to the floor. He peered around his room, his vision blurred from sleep. Everything, like his vintage posters of science-fiction movies and popular toy action figures, was still in place. Jacob's room contained every desire a twelve-year-old boy could have: a variety of gaming systems, a stereo, a big-screen television, and a gaming chair to navigate it all. A quick glance at the clock on his desk read three a.m.

Mama has to be home by now. What the hell was that noise?

He made his way into the darkened hallway and carefully stepped toward the kitchen. In the deafening silence, all he could hear was a high-pitched tone in his ears and the subtle whisper of his own breath. The length of the hallway appeared to stretch for miles. Nervous thoughts of an intruder wandering around the house caused his heart to race.

"Mom?" Jacob whispered. "Mom, are you there?"

The unexpected creak of the floorboard under his feet as he reached the end of the hall caused his heart to skip. Jacob pressed his chest against the wall and slowly peered around the edge of the corner into the kitchen. He scanned the area, and he noticed his mother's purse on top of the kitchen counter. He let out a sharp breath when he came out from behind the wall.

"Mama, what was that noise?" Jacob's heart raced as he searched the kitchen for his mother.

Outside the window over the kitchen sink, a man stared back at Jacob. Reginald's mouth moved quickly and rhythmically. His milky-white eyes were fixed as he glared. The man's sizable hands smacked against the windowpanes and caused the boy's body to jolt in terror.

Jacob screamed as he turned and ran back down the hallway. "Mama! Mama!" Screaming, he ran past his bedroom to his mother's. Connie's bedroom door quickly swung open and closed as she emerged, tying her robe. She grabbed her son by his shoulders and shook him until his screams ceased to fill the air.

"Son, what's wrong?"

"The neighbor, Mr. Reginald—I saw him through the window. His eyes looked creepy," he said.

She quickly walked to the kitchen and peered out the window. The area was calm, and nothing was on the other side but darkness.

The next morning, Jacob came out of his room for breakfast. His mom took special care to make his blueberry pancakes just the way he liked them. She devoted her time to make sure everything she made for him was perfect. His comfort was her highest priority.

"Hey, sweetie. How did you sleep?" Connie asked.

"Not great. I was afraid for most of the night. I know what I saw. What happened last night was not my imagination," Jacob replied.

"Honey, Mr. Reginald is harmless. He's just some old witch doctor who thinks all that mumbo jumbo is real. Just ignore him and any of his spooky stories dealing with that bayou. It's all superstition."

"Bayou?"

The doorbell rang, and Connie looked up in confusion. Jacob glanced in his mother's direction with the same confusion. No one had ever stopped by early in the morning. As a matter of fact, no one ever visited. They hadn't been in New Orleans long enough to have made any friends.

She noticed who it was when she looked through the blinds. "Umm ... give me a second," Connie spoke in a low voice, just loud enough for the person on the other side of the door to hear. She rushed to the rear doorway directly connected to the kitchen and opened the door.

The figure emerged from outside. The bright morning sunrise conflicted with the dark silhouette of the witch doctor. "Good morning. I wanted to check in with you. I heard the screaming last night, and I wanted to make sure everything was okay. I know we've started off on a little shaky ground, but I still want to keep my eye on you," Reginald said.

"Hey! Everything is great. Jacob just had a nightmare, and it was pretty intense. Thank you for checking on us," Connie replied.

Jacob averted his eyes as Reginald's glare lingered.

Reginald broke the few moments of silence that dawdled, clearing his throat. "Well, I can see everything is good here. I'll be on my way." Reginald quickly made his way to the rear doorway on his way out of the house.

"You know, we've been here a couple of weeks now, and you're still a stranger. It would be nice if we could get to know each other a bit more, don't you think, Reginald?" Connie approached him as he opened the door.

Reginald leaned back as she advanced closer. "I think you may be right. We're neighbors, and it would be natural for us to get to know one another a little better, to look out for one another." He closed the door. "Connie, I noticed you went for a leisure float on the bayou again."

"Of course. There's no way I wouldn't take advantage of a relaxing body of water right there in the back of our home. I wasn't going to let your rude outburst from our last encounter stop me. I'm not the docile type," Connie said.

"You may have noticed that the rest of us don't touch the bayou. You should be careful. There are hungry things that lurk in that water. You may have noticed that the water is much darker than the usual lake or bayou. It's unnatural," Reginald said. His eyes locked on Connie's.

"Hungry things?" Jacob asked.

Reginald turned and faced Jacob. "Gators and such. Don't worry. They rarely wander too close to the houses."

"Thank you for the concern. We'll keep that in mind. Jacob had a rough night, and we're trying to stay on time this morning. We have some errands to run. So if you don't mind," Connie said, holding the door open.

Reginald glared at Connie. "Stay away from the water."

Dusk settled in that evening. Jacob plopped himself on the couch after he finished some leftover homework and gnawed on his fingernails until he reached the flesh of his fingers.

Connie emerged from her bedroom. The heels of her stilettos had a rhythmic tap against the hardwood floor of the hallway as she made her way to the kitchen. The aroma of her perfume saturated the air as her red dress swayed from side to side. Her hands were busy adjusting her earrings to perfection.

"Where are you going?" Jacob asked, still chewing his nails.

"I have a date," Connie answered.

"A date?" Jacob stood up from the couch, eyes widened with confusion. "Mama, Daddy hasn't been dead for six months. Why are you going out with other men?"

"Son, you're young and I don't expect you to understand. I need to live my life. There's a pizza delivery on the way. I just want to go out and have a little fun. The money for the pizza is on the kitchen counter. Bed by eleven o'clock. I'll be back soon," Connie said. She barked her orders, oblivious to the shocked expression on Jacob's face.

"Mama, how could you be ready to date someone so soon?" Jacob pleaded. "This isn't right."

"Stop being dramatic. I won't be long. I just need to have some fun. Like I said before, I'll be back soon," Connie said. Her determined smile lingered as she left for the evening.

Hours passed, and Jacob slept on the couch, the television playing episode after episode of his favorite anime program. A paper plate with a half-eaten pizza crust rested on his stomach, and the flickering light from the television partially lit the darkened room.

A distant, high-pitched scream forced Jacob to snap out of his sleep. He stood, his chest heaving rapidly, eyes wide. Shadows darted along the walls from the still-flickering light. Unsure of where the scream originated, Jacob scrutinized the living room, stepping timidly toward the kitchen.

The rapid tapping on the window in the kitchen caught Jacob's attention. Reginald stood on the outside, his hands smacked against the glass. His eyes were again a milky white, and he held a knife with a jagged blade long enough to gut a large animal.

"You were warned," Reginald spewed, his hands firmly pressed against the window and his voice distorted.

Jacob screamed as he stared at the terrifying sight in front of him. Connie emerged from her room once again and sprinted down the hallway dressed only in her robe. Her look of concern was a universal sight among mothers at their children's screams. Connie watched as her son stood frozen in terror.

"Jacob! Jacob, what's wrong?" Connie shook his shoulders and tried to gain his attention.

"Mama, he's over there. He has a knife," Jacob yelled to his mother.

Connie scanned the kitchen to see what her son was screaming about. Everything was normal as usual. The lights were still off, and the television was still playing shows indiscriminately.

"Reginald. It was him. He was outside the window again. He had a knife, and his eyes were all freaky," Jacob said.

"Jacob, don't do this again. There's nothing here. No one is outside the window. I think you had a nightmare." Her eyes were vacant of the concern she displayed just moments ago.

"It wasn't a nightmare," Jacob yelled, his breaths labored. "I heard someone scream. Then I saw Reginald looking back at me through the window. I think he wants to kill me."

Connie exhaled sharply. "Is this because I'm going out at night? Jacob, I can't stay cooped up in this house. I need to go out and make friends."

"I didn't even know you were home. Fine, don't believe me. I'm going to bed."

Jacob used cardboard to cover every window in the house, excluding Connie's room, over the next week.

He clutched the large butcher's knife in his hand a little tighter, a little something he retrieved from the kitchen drawer earlier for comfort. It wasn't an ideal way for a twelve-year-old boy to spend his Saturday.

The entire week had been contentious with his mother. Connie's focus seemed elsewhere, with partying at the forefront just about every night. Jacob wanted nothing more than to have her home, protecting him from Reginald.

Jacob pulled a slight gap in the cardboard from the living room window and peered out over the fence at Reginald's backyard. The neighbor stood in the grass barefoot and shirtless, the dark water of the bayou behind him. Hideous scars covered his torso like a war-torn soldier. Jacob's heart thumped as Reginald glared back at the house. His body was still, and his eyes squinted as dusk settled in. The handle of the knife in Jacob's hand was wet with perspiration.

Jacob's nose burned as a stench filled the house over the last couple days. He had smelled nothing like it before. The repugnant odor soured his stomach.

"I don't know what your problem is, old man. I'm not going to let you hurt me or my mama. She may not think you're up to anything, but I know you're a monster," Jacob said.

After he taped the gap from the cardboard closed, Jacob tucked the knife into his pocket and sprinted to the kitchen and retrieved the sandwich and soda he had prepared earlier for dinner.

"Not sure when Mama's coming home. Better ride out the night in my room just to be on the safe side. I can lock the door and slide my desk in front of it. At least that way he can't sneak up on me."

Jacob slept in his gaming chair with his head resting

upon his desk and the knife still clutched in his hand. The discomfort of the unforgiving wood surface caused its share of strain on Jacob's neck. The sharp pain forced him to wake, and his eyes blinked rapidly from the light—there was no way he was sleeping with the lights off in his room. He checked the alarm clock on the nightstand.

"It's three a.m. Mama has to be home by now," he mumbled.

Jacob moved the desk, carefully opened the door, and peeked in the hall. He noticed a subtle orange hue emanating from under Connie's bedroom door. A slight grin crept onto his face as he exhaled in relief and stepped out of the room.

The smell he noticed earlier was stronger. Jacob held the back of his hand to his nose as his stomach soured from the stench. The knife in his hand felt heavy.

"Boy," a voice behind him whispered.

Jacob snapped his head over his shoulder. The silhouette of a large, darkened figure stood at the other end of the hallway, near the kitchen. The shirtless, muscular figure blended well in the low-lit area.

"Mr. Reginald, is that you? Why are you in our house?" Jacob asked. His voice was timid.

"I warned you. I warned both of you. You didn't listen," Reginald said as he stepped toward Jacob. "Come here." Reginald pulled the sharpened blade tucked in at the small of his back from his waistband.

Jacob's face cowed with terror at the sight of the large man approaching with a blade in his hand. Dropping the kitchen knife he held, Jacob's hands trembled in terror.

"Mama! Mama!" Jacob yelled. He backed toward Connie's bedroom door and banged on it until his fist throbbed with pain.

"Jacob, sweetie, what's wrong?" Connie stood in the doorway, partially dressed. Her tone was calm, unaffected by the panic that oozed from Jacob's yells.

Jacob gestured toward the dark shape at the hallway's end. The blade in Reginald's hand caught the light from Connie's room.

She pushed Jacob to the side at the sight of their neighbor's position at the end of the hall. Reginald's frame and aggressive stance awaited her as a hunter would stalk its prey. "You made a mistake coming in here, witch doctor." Her chest pulsated unnaturally. A subtle growl emanated from her throat.

"Jacob, come here, boy. Quickly!" Reginald pleaded, his hand reached out, sweat dripping from his brow. "Get your hands off the boy, demon."

Connie's body contorted. Her neck and skull narrowed and stretched as her fingers and nails lengthened and sharpened. The sound of her bones as they stretched and reshaped mimicked the sound of a butcher's cleaver as it chopped through flesh and slammed against the table.

"Mama? Mama, why does your face look like that?" Jacob asked. His voice trembled.

Jacob's eyes averted to inside Connie's well-lit bedroom. His heart thumped violently at the horror inside. A trio of partially rotted and dried-up corpses was stacked and intertwined in the room's corner. His brow raised at what he realized was the source of the screams he heard close by over the past week. Insects slithered their way along the mound of decay and feasted on the rotted flesh. The smell once again burned his nostrils as he inhaled the odor.

Connie glared down at him and bared her blackened teeth, pushing him into the bedroom.

"You won't hurt anyone again. I'll dump your body back in that cursed bayou, back where you came from," Reginald said, holding the blade in front of him. His muscles tensed as he stared at the beast in front of him. It was one thing to know the rituals and study the demon, but as its grotesque form stood in front of Reginald, it was different. His hands trembled slightly at the sight of her.

Connie sprinted toward Reginald. He stabbed her torso and pulled his blade back in almost one swift motion. Black liquid poured from her. Connie didn't make a sound. Reginald again sliced, across Connie's chest, again spilling more of what should have been blood from her. No sound. He leaped toward her and pressed the blade against her throat, slicing it open. Black blood poured from it as she stumbled back slightly. No effect.

Reginald froze as Connie plodded back toward him. He held the blood-covered knife in front of him. His intent was to sever the demon's head. Theoretically, he knew what needed to be done, but he had never encountered such a horrific beast in the flesh.

Connie sliced through the flesh of his extended arm. The blade he was holding fell to the floor. She seized him by the throat and hoisted him from his feet. Her moist, snake-like tongue slithered from her mouth and thrust its way into the back of his throat. His body thinned and his eyes bulged as she drained the life from him. He fell to the floor, brittle bones snapping, after she released him. Her tongue slithered its way back into her mouth, and her body shrank back to its previous form.

"Jacob, sweetie, it's safe to come out now. He can't hurt us anymore," Connie said, her voice warm and gentle.

Regardless of the corpses inside his mother's bedroom, Jacob hid inside near the entry after he saw the vicious acts of what he thought was Connie. He peeked around the door seal at his mother. His heart still thumped in his chest. "You killed him. You killed Mr. Reginald," Jacob said. He slowly emerged from her bedroom and stepped closer to her.

Connie grabbed Jacob and wrapped her arms around him, holding him close to her breast. "He was going to hurt you, baby. That evil witch doctor wanted to kill us both. I had to protect us."

"But your face—what happened to your face? And why are there dead bodies in your room?"

Connie extended her arms, holding Jacob away from her. The fear in Jacob's eyes made her brow furrow with concern, then it straightened as she grinned. "Don't concern yourself with it, sweetie. You've already seen too much."

Connie's body contorted, and her disfigured demon reappeared. Her hand was once again around another neck. She felt Jacob's heartbeat through her hand as she squeezed his throat. The succubus swiftly lifted him to eye level.

Jacob's final sight was his mother's horrifying face.

 The Swamp God

LM Kaplin

T roy let out a grunt as he twisted the hunting blade, forcing the sharpened tip through the thick hide. With a little elbow grease, the knife disappeared into the pale underside of the creature's neck, and a stream of blood seeped from the incision. The viscous liquid rolled along the slippery animal, staining the scaled skin a deep shade of red.

It took only a moment before the injured beast went limp in the water, bobbing with the waves alongside the chipped green paint of the boat's exterior. After the blow his brother had given it with the shotgun, the animal didn't put up much of a fight. Still, if Chet had better aim, his brother would have killed the creature with the first blast and saved him the trouble of getting up close and personal with the razor-toothed animal.

He looked at Chet and motioned for him to grab the other end of the beast as he struggled to haul the 400-pound alligator into the Air Ranger. As the brothers wrestled with the dead animal, Wayne pulled his Jon boat up alongside the other craft and slowed to a halt.

"You girls need sum help haulin' in yer catch?" he called over the bow.

Troy shot a glare back at his longtime friend. "I ain't see nothin' in yer boat 'cept a few empty beer cans," he called back to his hunting buddy as he heaved the gator over the hull, allowing it to drop with a thud onto the boat's deck next to a near-identical animal. The beast's weight rocked the craft back and forth in the murky water, sending Troy scrambling to regain his balance.

After steadying the boat, he inspected the pair of alligators and estimated how much he could sell them for back at the dock. The two similarly sized animals would likely fetch over a thousand dollars combined. The traps they had scattered throughout the swamp had paid off.

Wayne didn't give the brothers much time to relish their haul as he threw the accelerator forward, sending a wake toward the other craft. "Those run-o-the-mill gators in yer traps are barely worth getting out of bed for," he called back over his shoulder. "I got my eye on somethin' a bit more exotic."

Troy groaned. "Not with the albino alligator again."

Wayne had already traveled out of earshot, but his brother shook his head in disapproval. Chet made his way to the controls and fired up the large fan in the rear, sending a group of birds perched on a nearby cypress tree into the sky as the airboat propelled ahead.

When they were back within shouting distance, Troy called out, "Let's check the last couple traps. Then we can head home and get some lunch."

Wayne scowled and looked up at the sky. Although he wouldn't mind a sandwich, they had food in the cooler and the sun had yet to peak over the Louisiana bayou. Plenty of daylight remained for a trip deeper into the wetlands. He knew his companions would try to cut the outing short. They had lost the thrill of the hunt ages ago. Ever since being awarded their first gator hunting license through the state lottery, they cared only about making a quick buck. With beer money on the table, they had little appetite for chasing the legendary beast that the trio had been obsessed with as kids.

"Screw those traps. You'll never catch Parlangua in one of those," he said, evoking the historical name of a legendary local lizard. We got one more catch left on our permit this month. If we pick up another baby gator, what we gonna do when we find the one we've been searchin' for?"

"Since when has a permit ever mattered to you?" Chet yelled back with a chuckle, knowing his friend had never been one to abide by the rules.

"When we pull in with a two-million-dollar gator, there's gonna be a lot of attention on us. Last thing we need is the fish an' game warden confiscating our golden ticket on a technicality."

"Man, you gotta give up that dream," Troy called back. "We been looking for that albino gator since we first started combin' these waters."

"Damn it, Troy. I told you a hundred times, it ain't albino."

"Yea, yea. It's white, right? Then it's albino in my book," Troy replied.

"Whatever. You wouldn't understand the difference, anyway. The only thing you need to look for is the eyes. Albino gators have red eyes, but the one we're huntin' has eyes of sapphire. You see them blue peepers, you know it's her."

"If we ain't never seen one yet, they don't exist," Troy called back with confidence.

An involuntary laugh burst from Wayne's mouth at his friend's ignorant comment. "There's over three million acres of wetlands in Louisiana. The area we covered don't even amount to a drop in the bucket. There's prolly all sorts a things living out here that we ain't never seen."

The brothers glanced at each other with twin looks of resignation. There would be no convincing Wayne to head back early. Troy grabbed a couple of sandwiches from the cooler and tossed one to his brother.

"Lead the way, boss," Chet yelled. "But if we don't find yer white whale by three o'clock, we're headed back to check the last of the traps and sell our haul before the buyers close up shop for the day. Our beer fridge is runnin' low."

Wayne didn't need to be told twice. He threw the throttle forward, speeding ahead into the swamp. With just over three hours on the clock, he had no intention of wasting time combing the same areas they had been exploring their whole lives. If the ultra-rare alligators still existed, and he believed they did, they would have migrated away from human encroachment, into the deepest parts of the bayou.

Wayne had been waiting for the opportunity and came prepared for the trip. He had studied maps of the area, looking for the most likely spot to find the legendary creature. One particularly secluded area that was only accessible during the rainy season piqued his interest. With the successive storms that hit the area recently, the waters were at near the highest level they had ever been.

The group had never ventured that far into uncharted territory before. He wondered how long it would take before his buddies flagged him down to ask where they were going. Surprisingly, they traveled a good forty-five minutes before they attempted to garner his attention. Begrudgingly, he slowed down, ready to dismiss their concerns.

"What's the plan, chief?" Chet called out. "I thought we were goin' huntin', not burning gas on a joyride."

"Relax, bud," Wayne yelled back. "After our final catch, you'll have enough cash to fill yer tank a thousand times over. Just a little further southeast and we'll hit a spot where we can break for a spell. That's where we'll find her. You just watch."

As he prepared to continue forward, a movement caught the corner of his eye. His head snapped to the side, and he did a double-take at what he saw. Standing on the bank of the waterway was not the alligator he was hoping for, but a child. The boy looked to be no more than eight years old, though his emaciated body showed signs of prolonged malnutrition. He wore no shirt, just a thick layer of grime that covered his frail body. A set of pointed ribs jutted out from his chest so far it looked like the sharp bones would tear through the skin at any moment. The child wore only a tattered skirt made from what appeared to be a patchwork of old fabrics and animal skin. His calloused feet gripped the ground naturally, as if they had never known shoes. The boy's unsightly condition and feral appearance made Wayne wonder just how long the child had been wandering in the swamp and how he had survived in the wetlands.

Wayne prepared to call out to the boy, intending to ask if he needed help, although the answer to that question seemed obvious. But as he made eye contact with the child, who remained as motionless as a gator about to strike, something drew his gaze away from the boy's eyes and toward his mouth. Wayne strained his eyes, trying to understand what was wrong with the child.

Dark lines ran through his lips, discoloring the purple appendages.

At first, Wayne mistook the dark spots for rotten teeth, but as the boat drifted closer, he realized the truth was far worse. Thick, black stitches pierced the boy's lips. Each thread, driven deep into the swollen flesh and emerging on the other side, bound his lips together in a series of tight sutures. No wonder the boy was so emaciated. How could he eat with his mouth sewn shut? And who had done that to him?

Shocked by the unsettling sight, Wayne stumbled back, sending him off balance in the swaying boat. His foot slid across the aluminum deck, but just before falling overboard, he caught hold of the side rail. Through all the commotion, the boy didn't move. He didn't even flinch. He just stood rooted to the muddy bank, watching Wayne with a pair of pale-blue eyes.

Seeing the clamor in the other boat, Chet jerked the fan control so their airboat slowed to a low idle. The sudden drop in speed allowed the sounds of the bayou to consume the area. For a moment, they listened to the water slapping against the sides of the craft, the creak of branches rubbing together in the distance, and the occasional plop of something slipping beneath the water's surface.

"What the hell ya doin'?" Troy barked.

"Ya see that?" Wayne hollered, his voice cracking as he pointed toward the bank.

"Shit. Is that a kid?" Chet asked, squinting into the glare. "What's he wearin'? Some sorta skin?"

The boy tilted his head as if the words were sounds

he had never heard before. Flies buzzed around the corners of his mouth. His lips twitched around the stitches as if he wanted to speak, the black thread crimping the purple skin in jagged lines. The boy raised his hand and put a bony finger to his infected lips as if trying to shush the men.

"Hey!" Wayne bellowed, cupping his hands to his mouth. "Boy! You need help?"

The sound echoed across the calm water, bouncing between the trees. It carried farther than Wayne meant it to, silencing the nearby cicadas and birds.

The answer came swiftly, not from the boy, who had disappeared in an instant, but from the trees. A sharp, dry hiss whizzed by Wayne's ear. His head whipped to the side as realization hit him. He opened his mouth to yell, but before any sound escaped, a second arrow flew from the trees, landing a direct hit into his open mouth. The arrowhead erupted through the back of Wayne's neck as his yell turned into a pitiful gurgling sound.

He turned toward his companions, wide eyes bulging from his head, as bloody saliva leaked from his open mouth before tilting forward and falling headfirst into the water.

Without thinking it through, Chet dove in after his friend in an attempt to save him.

For a moment, Troy was alone. He stood on the edge of his craft, searching for any signs of life from his friends until movement in the bushes diverted his attention.

The branches parted, and figures emerged from between them, men and women painted head to toe in black mud. They were all half-naked, only wearing skirts similar to the child's. Their eyes remained focused on the intruders, and like the child, their mouths were each bound tightly with black thread, pursing their lips together into deformed puckers. Some held spears, tips emblazoned with jagged alligator teeth, pointed forward as if ready to strike.

A noise in the water behind him made Troy think of his friends. He spun toward the sound, but something snapped around his throat, biting into his skin. His hands went to his neck, frantically clawing to relieve the tension on his airway. Some sort of thick rope was digging into his skin, but he was unable to slip his fingers beneath the cord to ease the strain. He twisted his body desperately in an attempt to shake his attacker, but his vision faded as a blurry shape loomed over him, and he toppled overboard into the dark water below.

Troy woke to the high-pitched whine of mosquitoes buzzing in his ear. His skull throbbed in tune with the slow drip of water nearby. For a brief moment, he forgot where he was, until the burning sensation around his neck brought his memory rushing back.

He tried to reach up and massage his bruised throat, but his arms wouldn't budge. Looking down, he noticed thick vines wound around his bare shoulders and chest, binding him to a large tree emerging from waist-high water. He attempted to speak, to call out for help, but the sound caught in his throat and turned into a muffled grunt. His tongue felt thick inside his mouth, as if it had swelled to double its usual size. His lips were stiff and dry, each movement sent a sharp pain shooting through them. The throbbing prevented him from thinking clearly. Still groggy and confused, he tried to wet his lips, but his tongue couldn't reach them. With each movement, the taste of iron filled his mouth.

The image of the strange child and the black stitches binding his lips flashed through his head. He didn't need a mirror to know he had suffered the same fate. He winced as the memory returned, flashes of being held down by two men while a woman approached with a splintered fragment of bone in her hand. He had faded in and out of consciousness as the bone needle repeatedly pierced the tender flesh of lips.

Rage burned through his chest at the recollection, and he threw his weight to the side in an attempt to free himself. The tree's coarse bark dug deep into his flesh, sending pain screaming up his back. Ignoring the pain, he tried again, but the vines barely budged against his pull as he felt the trickle of a warm liquid running down his spine.

Facing the reality of his captivity, he thought of his companions. The image of Wayne with an arrow sticking out of his mouth and blood spewing from his open jaw flashed through his mind. The poor bastard. He wouldn't have survived that, especially not out there in the middle of the swamp. But where was his brother?

He craned his neck to each side, hoping to see Chet nearby but found only blankets of creeping moss and fallen logs rotting on the damp earth. Still, the possibility remained that his brother was near. He attempted to call for him, hoping even a muffled cry through his stitched mouth would be enough to garner Chet's attention. The threads tugged painfully when he tried to move his jaw, but for all his effort, only a pitiful murmur escaped his lips.

But somehow, an answer came to his failed call for help, because his brother emerged from behind the trees, running toward him at full speed. Upon seeing

Chet running free, Troy lit up with a renewed hope of freedom. Those aspirations were soon dashed as a group of irate natives pursued him out of the thicket.

Chet had no time to stop and untie his brother as his captors were only seconds behind him, but their eyes met for a moment and he offered his brother a grave look filled with sympathy and fear. Chet sprinted past the tree where Troy was bound, looking back over his shoulder at his pursuers.

With both hands, Chet dug into his mouth and ripped at the stitches, tearing his lips ragged in the process. The sound was grotesque, like a wet squelching noise as the flesh gave way. He unleashed a blood-curdling scream as his jaw freed itself from the bond. Shreds of his tattered lips hung limply from his mouth as his cries echoed through the bayou.

The effect on the tribe was immediate. They froze mid-step, their eyes flashing toward the black water nearby. One by one, they backed away, vanishing into the hanging moss. Seeing their retreat, Chet stopped, putting his hands on his knees to catch his breath and allow the pooling blood to flow freely from his ruined mouth.

Then, from the water came a sound. It was only a low bellow at first, not much different than a frog's mating call, but the intensity slowly increased. From the corner of his eye, Troy spotted a trail of ripples in the water as something moved below the surface.

His heart pounded in his ears. He tried again to scream, to warn his brother, but the threads held fast. Fresh blood filled his mouth, bitter and hot.

Then came a splashing sound as if something leaped out of the water. The source of the noise, and his brother, were out of his line of sight, but Troy didn't need to see what happened next to know the outcome. His brother's scream told him everything. It was the type of scream a man made only once in their lives.

Finally, an unnatural silence came over the swamp, broken only by the faint sound of running water in the distance and the rasp of Troy's ragged breath through his stitched lips. Then the sound returned—the alligator's deep bellow as it stalked its prey. It was circling him. He caught glimpses of it floating just beneath the murky surface, swimming in wide arcs yet closing in on him with each pass.

The tribe had vanished. He was alone. Alone with the thing that had swallowed his brother whole. And it was coming for him next. He finally found the mythical creature that swam through his dreams since he was a young boy but wouldn't live to tell the tale.

How many times had he pictured himself returning home with the beast in tow, earning accolades and untold riches from the rare catch? He knew at that moment that the opposite would be true. The article that detailed the disappearance of three missing alligator hunters wouldn't even mention the fabled creature. In truth, he didn't mind being gator food for such a magnificent animal, but the fact that Wayne, the most enthusiastic of the group, wasn't with him to share the encounter cast a shadow over the experience.

The water swelled, and a massive gator rose. Troy's heart sank when he saw the green scales break the surface, realizing it wasn't the exotic white gator after all. But when the animal should have reached its peak height, the beast continued to rise, up and up, until it stood on two legs, towering over him. The swamp god, Parlangua, a creature so fabled they had never even believed it existed, stood before him.

Clumps of mud and lilies clung to its scaled body as the beast rose to its full height. Half man and half gator, the monster defied the laws of nature. With no means to fight or flee, Troy accepted that he would meet his end and mumbled a prayer. He expected the creature to bend down and bite off his head, ending his life in one swoop, but instead, the beast reached for him.

Its claw curled around his bicep, and its sharp nails dug into his soft muscle. With a sickening crunch, it tore the limb free. Troy tried to scream, but with his mouth sewn shut, he was unable to satisfy the urge. A geyser of blood erupted from his shoulder, pulsing in rhythm with his faltering heartbeat.

He could only watch in shocked horror as the creature put his arm to its mouth and stripped the meat away as it cleaned the bone like a man gnawing on a chicken wing. When it finished, it flicked the remaining tangle of bone and gristle to the ground, where they landed with a clatter at Troy's feet.

Luckily for him, he passed out before the beast came in for a second helping.

THE GRUNCH

ERIC BUTLER

"**W**ell, last night was disappointing," Gail said, slipping into the last seat at the table.

Anna's eyebrows rose. "I don't know. From what I could hear coming through the hotel wall, it sounded like you and Frank ended it with a bang."

Gail rolled her eyes, ignoring the laughter coming from the others and the rush of heat to Frank's cheeks as he sat down next to her. Her husband was such a prude sometimes. "Bitch, you damn well know I mean the ghost tour."

"Anna's just upset 'cause her friend is in town," Kevin said.

"Yeah, we all got here ..." Frank trailed off, suddenly understanding. His cheeks grew redder.

"Jesus Christ," Gail said, her hand going under the table to rest on his knee. She resisted the urge to squeeze.

Penny gave Frank a sympathetic glance before taking

a sip of her orange juice. Everyone knew Penny never liked the way her sister treated Frank—everyone except Frank. "I met a guy at the bar last night. Called himself Voodoo Vinny. He promised me a night to remember."

"And?" Anna asked, a wicked grin on her face. "Was it?"

"I guess we'll find out tonight," she replied. She pulled her arms back, making space for the waitress to set down the full plate of beignets they ordered. "He said for five hundred bucks he'd take us on a tour that would scare the curls out of my hair ... up top *and* down low."

Frank practically glowed.

"Ah shit, honey," the waitress said. "Y'all better be careful. Vince ain't right in the head."

Gail's head snapped up, her mouth opening to chastise the woman, but her sister spoke first.

"What do you mean? He seemed authentic enough."

"Vinny grew up deep in the bayou, and from the sounds of it, he's offerin' to take you to Grunch Road," she said with a shake of her head.

Penny nodded. "Yeah, that's the place he mentioned. Said we'd see something unforgettable."

A wordless cry pulled the waitress's attention from the group, and she reached out to place a hand on Penny's shoulder. "Ain' no one needin' to go there, no how."

"What's Grunch Road?" Kevin asked, his eyes following the waitress as she disappeared back into the crowded room.

Penny shrugged. She grabbed the powdered-sugar covered donut and held it before her lips. "No idea, but Vince said tonight was the best time to see it. Whatever *it* is." She took a bite, chewed in silence, then swallowed before continuing. "It's up to y'all, but I think we should go. He said to meet him at the Pump and Go parking lot off Morrison tonight at nine o'clock."

"A gas station parking lot in New Orleans," Kevin said, reaching for a beignet. "What could go wrong?"

The van rolled to a stop, and the driver glanced back over his shoulder. "Are y'all sure y'all want to get out here?"

Penny looked out the window, resisting the urge to say no. The whole place was in shadows, the only light coming from the moon overhead and the soft glow of neon lights through the front window of the building. There were two pumps, but neither looked like they had worked since the early eighties. Looking at the dilapidated building and the cracked asphalt of the parking lot, she suddenly wondered if the waitress had been right. *This might not be such a good idea.*

"Is he even here?" Gail asked.

Before anyone could answer, a streetlight flickered on and bathed a figure in light. Penny blinked. It looked like the same guy from the night before, but something was different. He was taller and thicker than she remembered. He wore khakis, dark boots, and an army-green T-shirt under a camouflaged jacket with the sleeves cut off. His arms bulged with muscles she didn't quite remember seeing at the bar.

"Is that a machete?" Frank asked, pointing at the sheath dangling from the man's hip.

The driver cleared his throat. "Again ... are y'all sure you want to get out here?"

Gail grabbed the handle and pulled the door open.

"This is already way better than that lame ghost tour. Let's go see what Penny's mysterious man has to offer."

Kevin held out a twenty to the driver. "Do me a favor and wait here for a few minutes in case we change our minds. I'll give you a wave if we decide to stay."

The man plucked the cash from Kevin's hand with a nod. "It's y'all's funeral."

"Ah *chere*, I was hopin' I'd see ya tonight," the man said as they walked up. He offered them a wide smile and threw his arms out. "And ya brought friends."

They stopped short, keeping a few feet between them and the man. After a moment of hesitation, Frank stepped forward and introduced everyone. The man's head bobbed in the direction of each person when Frank spoke their name.

"Good evenin', folks. I'm sure the lovely Ms. Penny told y'all, but jus' in case, I be Vincent D'oobache. Some call me Vinny, others Vince, and to the uninitiated, I been called Voodoo Vince from time t' time. After tonight, w'all be family, so y'all call me whatever ya heart desires."

"Okay, Vinny," Gail said with a crooked grin. "How about you tell us what exactly you plan on showing us for our money."

Vince placed his hand over his heart. "*Ma petite*, straight t' de point. Ima gonna show ya somethin' civilized folks forgot eons ago. Sometin' that'll make ya blood run cold and da hair on ya arms stand at attention."

"See?" Penny said, patting her sister on her shoulder. "I told you it would be better than the ghost tour."

"An' cheaper, t' boot," Vince said with a wink. "Are y'all brave nuff t' witness de scariest thing of y'all's lives?"

Kevin raised his hand and waved to the driver. The van's headlights flashed once, and he pulled away.

"I reckon dat's a yes," Vince said. He held out his hand. "I hate t' be crass, but I mus'   insist for de t'ree hun'red upfront. Folks tend to grow forgetful once de shit hits de fan, so t' say."

"So does this night of terror start here?" Kevin asked, looking around. "I mean ... it's just an abandoned gas station."

"Very true, *mon ami*," Vince said, closing his fist as soon as Penny put the cash on his palm. "On both accounts. It do be abandoned, and our night of adventure shall *begin* here. Just not de way y'all are expectin'."

Anna groaned when he pointed at her shoes. "Oh god, how far?" she asked, cursing herself for wearing heels.

"If we survive de night, ya need t' put some money down on de ponies, *chere*," Vince said, squatting down to pull a pair of black rubber boots out of his pack. "Lady luck smiles upon ya."

"No one said anything about walking," she grumbled, stepping over to take the offered rubbers. She turned and rested her hand on Frank's shoulder to balance herself as she took off her shoes. She slipped on the boots and clicked her heels. "A perfect fit. Maybe we do need to hit the track."

Vince slung his pack over his shoulder, then pointed toward the line of trees back behind the station. "On t' other side of dos trees is de t'ing y'all've been seekin' in N'arlons."

"Oh yeah?" Penny asked, walking past him and toward the trees. "And what's that?"

"T' feel truly alive, a'course."

Vinny led them through the trees and stopped by a chain link fence. He stood under a sign that read No Trespassing and clearly stated what would happen to anyone who ignored the warning.

"I guess this is part of the adventure you've been promising us?" Frank asked, motioning to the sign.

Vinny glanced up, saw the sign, and chuckled. "*Oui bien, sûr,*" Vinny said, flashing a wide smile and reaching down to grab the fence with both hands. He pulled it back, exposing an opening large enough for a person to slip through. "But mos'ly, it's t' remind me where I put de doorway."

Gail laughed, a quick bark of mirth, and patted Frank on the shoulder. "Live a little," she said, stepping to the opening. She paused and glanced over at Vinny, studying his face. Half of it was hidden in the night's shadow, but the part she could see she found oddly comforting.

"If this is all you've promised, I'll double your fee. But if this is some snipe hunt ..." She let the unspoken threat hover between them for a few seconds before stepping through the opening.

The ground felt softer on that side of the fence. *Spongier.* Gail slid to the side, making sure there was enough room for the others as they slipped through the fence. Vinny went last, letting the fence fall back into place.

"Good as new," he said, stepping over to stand in a beam of moonlight. "And now de fun begins. We are on de edge of de Bayou Sauvage Urban National Wildlife

Refuge. All dis used t' be open for everyone to wander, but sumtin happened back when I was no more dan a tadpole—sumtin so scary dey made all dis to hide it."

"And what was that?" Anna asked, sliding closer to hug Kevin's left arm. He reached over with his free arm and patted her hand.

Vinny reached into his pack and pulled out a lantern. He twisted the top and pulled it up, bathing them all in the soft glow of artificial light. Stepping closer, he raised the lantern so his whole face was illuminated. He offered them a toothy grin.

"Da Grunch, a'course."

The sounds of the bayou stopped suddenly as if Vinny somehow had a way to pause all the insects, nocturnal beasts, and even the water. The group gazed toward the darkness, their wide eyes shiny in the moonlight. Then, just as quickly as it stopped, the noises began anew.

"Neat trick," Gail grumbled.

"What's a Grunch?" Frank asked, looking around to see if the bayou grew quiet when he said the word. A disappointed look settled on his face when it didn't. Penny patted him on the shoulder.

Vinny held out the lantern for Gail to take. He reached into his bag and pulled out another. "Some t'ink the Grunch are a tribe of man-eating humanoids dat live out here, but dey be wrong. It's sumtin burped straight outta Hades, but a beastie non'-de-less."

"What the hell?" Kevin blurted out.

"Exactly," Vinny said with a wink. He held out the other lantern, shaking it in Frank's direction when no one made a move to take it.

A loud splash sounded off in the darkness, and Anna let out a squeak. "Nuthin' to fear, *chere*. Dat is jus' de chariot I promised y'all."

A light flared in the middle of the darkness, revealing a man guiding a flat-bottomed boat with a pole. He waved, and Vinny raised his hand in return. "At the helm is my cousin, 'Enry. He'll get us dere in two shakes of a lamb's tail."

The boat glided across the water. Frank stood near the bow and held out the lantern. He squinted into the darkness and wondered why he let himself get talked into these "adventures." His whole body was tensed up, ready to spring into action at the first sign of trouble, although listening to Vince go on about a made-up creature had him wondering exactly what he would be able to do if it did show up.

Supposedly, they were headed to see a creature the size of a rottweiler, with a large wooly mane and covered in a thick, scaly hide. Add in the long snout filled with teeth, glowing, red eyes, and elongated limbs with razor-sharp claws at the end, and one thing was for sure—if it wasn't all a bunch of hogwash, Gail would be happy. He let out a long sigh. *Which is why you let yourself get talked into these little adventures of hers.*

A splash sounded off to the left. *Port side*, he thought with a nod. He swung the lantern in that direction and straightened up when the light reflected off shiny orbs at the water's surface.

"Are those ...?" Anna's question trailed off, and she swallowed.

"Don' y'all worry none," Vinny said from the stern of the craft. "Dey just curious, is all."

"Probably smell de goat," Henry said.

As if on cue, a sharp cry sounded from under a thick, dark blanket.

"What do you mean goat?" Penny asked.

Vinny reached down and pulled the blanket up to reveal a small goat inside a cage. It cried out again.

The mournful sound sent a shiver down Frank's back. "Why do you have a goat?"

"Yeah, Vincent," Penny said, squatting down to stick her fingers inside the bars. "Why *do* you have a goat?"

"Ah, *chere*. I wouldn'-"

The goat snapped at her fingers, drawing blood. "Shit," she cried out, snatching her hand back and holding it to her chest. "That thing bit me."

Vinny dropped the blanket back over the cage and offered her a sympathetic smile. "I tried t' warn ya. Billy is a right bastard."

"Yeah, I give 'im a fifty-fifty chance wit' da Grunch," Henry added.

"Wait," Kevin said, holding out a handkerchief for Penny. "You've seen it too?"

"Why do ya t'ink I asked fer five hun'red?" Vinny said with a chuckle. "Dis scaredy cat won' come for less, and he refuses t' leave de boat."

"Not enough money in da world for dat," he said, shaking his head.

The boat slid to a stop, the edge bumping into the marshy shore. Vinny tied the boat to a thick wooden post jutting from the water and then hopped off. He turned to face the group. "Before de swamp reclaimed what was hers, dis use t' be Grunch Road. Soon y'all will see de true face a terror."

Henry offered a grunt and pulled the goat from the cage. He slipped a thick loop of rope over its head before holding it out. Vinny grabbed the animal, then took a few steps back, motioning with a nod of his head that the others should follow.

After everyone got off the boat, Vinny cleared his throat. He waited until everyone was looking at him. "Dis is where we bid *adieu* to poor 'Enry for a bit. We wan' each and every one a y'all t' see him agin, so I need y'all ta listen up. If ya changed yer   mind, we'll think no less a ya. Plenty a space on de boat to wait. Understan'?" He paused and looked each person in their eyes until they nodded. "Good. Now de hard part. Y'all must do as I tell ya and follow where I walk. When we get dere, we gonna watch de beastie from a large cage. Keep yer hands inside at all times."

"A cage?" Gail asked, her head slightly tilted.

"If we could watch from de boat, we'd do dat, but dere is only one spot da Grunch will show itself," Vinny said with a shrug. He raised his free arm and pointed toward a cluster of trees and undergrowth at the end of the path. "And dat's in dere."

"But if we have to get in a cage, how do we get back to the boat safely?" Anna asked, glancing around with wide, unblinking eyes.

Vinny patted his bag. "Dey always been scared a loud noises. Dey'll scamper off from what's in dis bag."

"Reminds me of when you dragged us to that wildlife enclosure in Texas," Frank said. "Can we take pictures?"

"But of course, *mon ami*," Vinny said with a toothy grin. "Get yer money's worth. Now, if y'all be ready, let's go, single file. One light up front and de other in de back."

"Stay on de path. Ya don' wanna fall in dese waters no

how," Henry called out as they walked away from the boat and into the trees.

Penny noticed the path squished under her steps and sprung up as her foot lifted. It made her think of the astronauts walking on the moon, and she fought the urge to see if it might make her jump higher than usual. Her eyes darted over to the dark surface of the water, and Henry's words echoed in her head. *He's right. I don't want to fall in there.*

A splash to the left pulled her attention to the other side of the path. They were surrounded by water. *And everything lurking under it.* She shivered at the thought. If only she had kept it to herself, but she knew how disappointed Gail was with the trip so far. *Hell, even if this ends without us seeing anything, this part has to have given her the thrill she's been seeking.*

The path disappeared into a line of trees. She glanced back, trying to find the boat but unable to see anything past Kevin and the lantern. Just darkness. She couldn't help but think she should go back. *Maybe we all should.*

"Can't get cold feet now," Kevin said, gesturing forward. "Let's go see this 'monster' so your sister is happy and I can get back to the bar."

Penny nodded and stepped into the grove. The path widened, spreading out until the edges disappeared into the darkness. More trees dotted the area, spread out haphazardly and making it seem more maze-like than it probably would have in the daylight. Vinny continued forward, drifting left or right depending on the undergrowth. Gail stayed close behind him, offering the light from her lantern when the moonlight above was blocked. Her head swung back and forth, searching for the monster promised them.

The party came upon a wall of foliage, vines, and branches flowing together to bar their path. Vinny motioned for Gail to step to the left and lower her lantern. At first, Penny didn't understand what they were staring at, but when she leaned closer and really looked, a dark opening appeared. It was small, no higher than four feet and just wide enough to let the largest of them pass through.

Vinny squatted down and scurried into the darkness. His voice drifted back to the group. "Hurry up, now. Y'all don' wanna be outside dos' cages when our visitor arrives."

Gail scurried after him, then Frank and Anna followed. Penny watched Anna in envy as she simply squatted and walked through the tunnel of growth. Sighing, she dropped to her hands and knees and crawled. The ground was damp, slippery in places, and she grimaced every time her hand came down on something slimy. She could see the light from her sister's lantern ahead, and though it felt like they were crawling forever, she popped up on the other side in less than a minute.

They stood in a large opening. Moonlight shone down, and though it offered some illumination of the clearing, there were still quite a few pockets of shadows. Vinny knelt in the middle and tied the goat to a chain wrapped around a large hunk of stone. A long cage sat on its side and reminded Penny of the ones used underwater to watch sharks. It was tall enough for every one of them to stand and wide enough that they could fit a few more people in before it would have been considered crowded.

On the other side of the clearing, there were two obvious paths doused in inky-black shadow. She could only assume they disappeared deeper into the swampy marsh around them. Vinny stood and motioned for Gail and Kevin to come over and hang their lanterns on two poles positioned near the large stone. The two lanterns added to the natural moonlight and chased the shadows back.

The goat tested the rope, crying out when it reached the end.

"Hurry now," Vinny said, pulling the long bolt from the cage's latch. He pulled the door back and held it while they entered the cage. "Don' forget t' get ready t' take ya pi'tures. When de beastie comes, he comes fast."

Penny stood at the opposite end, her shoulder pressed against the hard steel bars. Her gaze darted down and found another large bolt slid into a catch to hold a smaller trapdoor closed. She reached down, her fingers circling the bolt's head, and tried to pull it free. It didn't budge, and she wondered if it might be rusted in place or simply jammed.

The shrill cry of rusty hinges pulled her attention back to the other end and most likely answered her question. Vinny slipped the bolt into place and tested the door to make sure it couldn't just be pulled open. He caught Penny's gaze and flashed a smile.

"Better safe dan sorry, *chere*."

"How long do we have to—" Frank's question cut off with a gasped breath.

Gail pulled her shirt over her nose. "Jesus Christ, what is that smell?"

Penny tried to ignore the gagging sounds coming from Anna and Kevin and concentrated on keeping her dinner down. The smell was intense, so thick and heavy it seemed to coat her tongue. For a moment, she struggled to place it, but then it hit her. *Just like when the skunk sprayed poor old Jasper.* She grimaced at the memory, still amazed they were able to get the smell out of his fur. *But it's not just that.*

No, there was more to it, something musky. *Something filthy?* She shook her head. *No, that's not it … something rotten.* The goat screamed, not in frustration but pure terror. Penny's head snapped up, her gaze locking onto two glowing, red eyes watching them from the shadows. Icy fear sent a shiver down her back and made her insides squirm.

"Holy shit," Frank said, his voice wavering. "This is real?"

Penny knew she should pull out her phone and hit record, but instead, she stood frozen as the creature stepped into the light. It was exactly as Vinny described it to them and yet somehow worse. She struggled to breathe, the putrid stink growing stronger. *How is that possible?* She wanted to tear her gaze from the beast or, at the very least, cover her eyes, but instead, she watched with wide, shiny eyes as it approach the goat.

The goat screamed again, twisting and tugging its head in a wild attempt to get free from the rope. The beast lunged forward and raked its razor-sharp claws across the goat's side. Blood rushed from the wound, gushing through the slashes to spill on the ground with a splash. The Grunch pulled the still-screaming animal closer and buried its snout into the bloody gash.

No one spoke. The goat gave one last shrill cry and then fell silent. All Penny could hear was the beast slurping and lapping up the blood. Anna hunched over and heaved. Vomit spewed past her lips and through the bars. The Grunch threw back its head and sniffed before swinging its gaze over to the cage.

"Oh shit," Gail whispered. The Grunch dropped the carcass and rushed toward the cage. She kept her phone on the creature but reached over with her free hand to tug on Anna's shirt. "Straighten up."

"Come on, honey," Kevin barked.

He reached down to grab her. His phone slipped from his fingers and fell to the ground, landing in the pool of vomit with a splat. Before she could straighten, the Grunch slashed out and drove its claws into the back of her neck. Blood squirted from the wound and splashed down to mix with her vomit. Anna released a startled squeak that quickly shifted to a shriek as its claws raked over her scalp.

The force of the attack pulled her forward, and her head slammed against the thick metal bars. Her cry cut short, and she tumbled to her knees, landing in the bloody vomit stew beneath her. Anna threw her hands to the back of her head, pressing them tightly against the wounds in a desperate attempt to stop the bleeding.

The Grunch swung again, that time from below. Its claws bit into her chin and sliced upward, opening her face. She screamed a gurgled, bloody cry for help, but everyone just stood frozen. The creature jerked Anna closer and wedged her head between two bars. Its lips pulled back, and Penny's eyes widened at the sight of all its teeth.

The creature bit down on the back of Anna's head and drove its teeth into her skull, splitting it open to expose her brain. A long, thin, purplish tongue wormed into the wound, and it slurped out chunks of the pink meat inside. Anna's body spasmed, and she released a low, gurgled sigh. Kevin cried out and grabbed his wife's shoulders. The Grunch issued a throaty growl, but Kevin ignored it and tried to pull her free.

The beast roared, its cry more of a shriek than a howl. The sound washed over Penny and drove all the warmth from her body. Kevin's hands slipped from his wife, a wet stain growing on the crotch of his pants. The scent of hot urine mixed with the beast's stench, and Penny's stomach rolled.

"Do something!" Gail screamed, jabbing her finger toward Vinny.

He dug through his bag and jerked out an old-fashioned alarm clock.

"What the fuck is that?"

Vinny began to wind the key in the back. "I told y'all. De Grunch hates noise. Dis mak-"

The word cut short with a gasp. Blood ran from the corners of his gaping mouth. The clock slipped from his hands, but all Penny saw was the bloody arm jutting from his chest. It was long and muscular, its hair matted with gore. Clutched in its fist was Vinny's still-beating heart.

"There's another one?" Frank said, his normally quiet voice a few octaves higher.

"Get the clock," Penny hollered, diving at Vinny's feet.

The beasts roared in unison when Penny's fingers wrapped around the clock. Trembling, she tried to ignore the icy ball of fear growing in her belly and frantically   searched for the key. Blood rained down on her. At first, it was just a few drops, but then a flood of hot, sticky, red gore splashed down over her back and neck. Gail screamed something, but if it was a warning, Penny didn't understand. Not until Vinny's heart fell next to her face with a meaty thump.

Penny tried to rear up, but Vinny's body slammed onto her and drove her back to the ground. The air whooshed from her lungs, and the clock slipped from her grip. Stars danced before her, and she struggled to catch her breath. She watched as the second beast reached through the bars and snatched up the clock.

Frank wrestled the dead guide off Penny and pulled her to her feet.

"You okay?" he asked, turning the last syllable into a wordless howl as his face scrunched up in pain.

The first Grunch reached through the bars, swiping its arm back and forth. Its claws tore through Frank's right pants leg and sliced through his Achilles. Penny wrapped her arms around him, desperate to keep him upright.

"Kevin, help," she gasped out when it became apparent she couldn't keep Frank up. When no one arrived to help, Penny glanced back and found him rolled up in the fetal position. "Goddamn it, man, HELP ME."

He didn't move, but Gail slid next to her and helped support her husband's weight. "I've got him, but what are we gonna do?"

"I don't know," Penny answered through gritted teeth. "Do you really?"

"Yes."

Penny let go, bracing in case she needed to help keep him upright. When he didn't crash down on her, she hunched over and snagged Vinny's back. "I don't know ... maybe there's something in here."

She turned the bag upside down and dumped the contents onto the ground. She could see a phone, Vinny's wallet, pliers, and what looked like an oversized plastic gun.

Frank grabbed her attention with a sharp hiss. "Flare gun," he gasped out, the pain evident in his voice.

Before she could ask any questions, a loud screech

of metal sounded behind her. Penny snatched up the flare gun and slipped to the other side of Frank. The two women helped maneuver him to the other end of the cage. A Grunch stood at the opening, the cage's door clutched in one taloned grip, the bolt in the other.

"Jesus," Gail moaned. "Are these things ... smart?"

"Not smart enough," Penny answered, raising the gun to take aim. She prayed it was loaded, then pulled the trigger. The flare shot across the cage and slammed into the creature's face. It howled in pain, and the hot sparks of the flare ignited the beast's hair. The fire burned hot, melting the Grunch's eyes and charring its face. It scurried back, holding the door open until the last possible moment.

The first Grunch slipped past its burning brother and sprang upon Kevin's trembling figure. The other let loose the door and tumbled to the ground. It no longer made any noise save a few desperate mews until the flames engulfed its entire body and it grew quiet.

Kevin's screams filled her ears, and the creature's stench brought tears to Penny's eyes. She wished to block out his cries but instead focused on clearing her vision.

The other Grunch ignored them, raking its claws across Kevin's body until it was soaked in his blood. It buried its snout in his chest, cracking through his ribs and pushing deeper to feed on his insides.

Penny scrambled to the pliers, wincing when the beast grumbled at her movement. She braced herself for its attack, but when it didn't come, she snatched them up. "Come on," she hissed at her sister, who helped Frank hobble to the opposite side of the cage.

Penny grabbed the head of the bolt with the pliers, working it back and forth.

"What are you doing?"

"If I get the bolt free," she said, the words rushing out between frustrated grunts,   "we might have a chance to get back to the boat."

"Maybe we can trap it in this cage," Frank mumbled, his eyes dull from the blood loss. "'Cause I don't think I'm going far without a lot of help."

Penny nodded. "Yeah, even better. We trap this thing and then I can go get 'Enry to help."

"If that asshole is even still there," Gail grumbled.

Penny let out a wordless cry and held the bolt up for them to see. She pushed on the door, but it didn't move.

Frank pulled away from Gail and staggered to the door. He slammed into the bars and pushed with all his strength, but the door remained shut.

The beast growled. Penny glanced back and whimpered.

"Push," Gail shouted, slipping next to her husband to add her strength. "Hurry."

All three pushed, and just when Penny thought they should give up, the door shifted. The hinge squealed in protest, but the door swung out. When it opened enough to allow them space to exit, Frank pressed his hand against Gail's back and pushed. She tumbled to the ground outside.

"If I can get the machette, I'll hold it off," he barked at Penny, grabbing her arm and slinging her after her sister. "You get her to the boat."

The creature roared, and Frank spun around just in time to catch it in his arms. His injured leg slammed back into the bars, and he screamed in pain.

Penny scrambled to her feet, tugging on her sister's arm to get her off the ground. She watched her brother-in-law's legs buckle under the weight of the squirming beast and tumble back to wedge himself in the opening. The Grunch's maw spread wide, and Penny's stomach rolled at the sight of Kevin's flesh stuck between its teeth.

"RUNNNNN—" Frank's cry cut short when the Grunch's jaws snapped shut around his throat.

"Oh god," Gail whimpered, weakly reaching in her husband's direction.

Penny began to run, jerking on her sister's arm to get her to follow. The two ran from the cage toward the wall of foliage, Penny's head shifting back and forth while she searched for the opening. *Where is it?*

The creature howled.

"Don't look back," she said, the words choked with emotion. She swallowed, knowing it wasn't the time to dwell on their nightmare. Her gaze swept over a dark shadow. She snapped her attention back to the spot. "There," she barked, and dove into the opening.

Penny waited until she felt her sister's hand press against her backside before scrambling through the tunnel on her hands and knees. Though the tunnel was pitch black, she could see moonlight shining down ahead. They were close. She had no idea if Henry would wait around after all the noise those monsters made or if he even heard any of it. *Please still be there.*

She burst from the opening and sprang to her feet, reaching back to help her sister up. Gail grabbed her hand.

"We need to go back," she whimpered. "He might still be ..." She let the sentence trail off and, instead, pleaded with her eyes.

"Honey, we don't have time," Penny cooed. "We'll come back with help, but first we need to get on the boat."

A roar echoed from the tunnel, and Gail's hand slipped from Penny's grip. Her body shuddered before jerking back into the darkness. Her scream cut short, and all Penny could hear was a gargled moan and the sounds of tearing flesh. Tears ran down her cheeks, and she turned to run toward the boat, but what she saw made her heart drop. *No.* Henry was using the pole to guide the boat away.

"Stop," she cried out. "Please. I'm still here." She sped up and raced down the path, but the boat continued to drift farther away.

Henry glanced back over his shoulder and offered her a slight shake of his head. "I will light a candle for ya dis very night," he called out. "But dey can't swim, and I ain't comin' back."

"Goddamn it," Penny screamed, pulling up as she approached the end of the path.

Her knee buckled when her foot came down on the spongy growth covering the path, and she tumbled to the ground. The Grunch shrieked again, announcing it was on her side of the tunnel. She rolled over and threw her arms up in a weak attempt to protect herself. Maybe she could have fought it off.

She opened her mouth to scream at the beast, but nothing came out but a startled squeak as the creature rushed past her to leap toward the flat-bottomed craft. She cried out in pain as the Grunch's back claws sliced up her arm and drew blood. She continued to roll, stopping when she lay on her stomach. She watched with wide eyes as the beast soared through the air and landed on the edge of the boat.

Henry squealed and tried to swing the pole to knock the Grunch from his boat. It hopped up, easily dodging the awkward attack, and slashed its claws across the man's belly. His insides poured out to land on the deck with a wet splat. The creature slurped up his guts, chomping on Henry's entrails and swallowing them down.

The swamp around her grew quiet, the only sounds being the monster's feeding and Henry's cries.

Penny watched the boat drift farther away, both grateful and terrified by the implications. The monsters were gone—*for now*—but so was her way back to civilization. She wondered if her phone had any bars, and though she wanted to check, she realized she wasn't moving. *So tired*. She took a shuddered breath and forced her gaze to her arm.

Blood gushed from the wound and splashed into the swamp. *Need to stop the ble-* She didn't finish her thought, suddenly aware of the eyes watching her from the water. They gently bobbed at the surface a few feet away. In her mind, she told her arm to move, told her whole body to do something, but nothing happened—nothing   but the eyes gliding closer.

Sharp teeth dug into her wrist and dragged her into the murky, brown water. Penny remembered reading that alligators liked to drown their victims. After seeing how the Grunch killed, she hoped that was true. *If only we had listened to the waitress*, she thought, the woman's words echoing in her head as the water rushed into her open mouth.

Ain' no one needin' to go there, no how.

HOMEGOING

R.J. JOSEPH

I had been alone there in the bayou for so long I almost did not recognize the pale face staring at me through the hanging moss. Perhaps I should not call my state aloneness. I had the trees, which sang to me every night. I had the slight humid breeze that gave the trees voices to speak. The animals comforted me when I could not remember my life before the swamp.

But she was the first human I had ever seen in the entire time home.

She and I stared at one another for long moments before I raised my hand in greeting. She started with halting steps toward me. I noticed the rips in her odd clothing, the blood pouring from her head. I rushed to her, then, so she would not further injure herself.

We walked slowly to my cabin, the lone structure for many miles, surrounded by the murky bayou I called home. The space was silent as we passed through, my usual company keepers reverent of our trek. Even our footsteps on moist foliage muffled out of respect for our solemn journey.

Neither of us spoke as I sat her down at the table and drew water to clean and inspect her wounds. I wiped away layers of blood and dirt and plant matter. The hole in the back of her head did not shock me as much as her ability to remain functional with a quarter of her skull and its contents missing.

"Are you ... in pain?" It was an inane thing to ask; still, I uttered the words.

Her only answer was a shuddering breath that sounded like it emanated from her very soul.

I bound her head lightly with rags from a torn sheet. She bled no longer, but I covered a pillow in extra rags, just in case. She followed me around the settee and sat when I motioned her to do so.

I cleaned the kitchen area and readied myself for bed. The other girl sat motionless on the settee. Before I blew the lantern out, I caught a glimpse of her eyes, lowered as if she could not wait to sleep but haunted enough that I doubted she would.

She and I spent long days with her following me around the bayou and around the cabin. I had taken to simply keeping up my regular conversations with the birds rather than trying to get her to talk. After the first few days, her right eye became covered with a cloudy gray film, which did nothing to significantly alter her looks or her ability to see whatever she needed to see. She followed my voice when I addressed our sistren throughout nature. Her footsteps never faltered as we navigated the winding roots of the water hickory and trumpet creepers swaying in the breeze. She also never questioned how I knew their names or whether they spoke back to me.

After a point of time I could not determine, our daily walk farther into the woods brought us to a pale girl sitting against a tree, almost covered by the moss and water hyacinths surrounding her. We exchanged a glance and silently moved in unison to investigate our new visitor.

The third girl jumped up as we approached her, hugging my companion first and then me. Her eyes were wild, and she smelled more strongly of the fresh, mossy water than I was used to.

"Oh my god! I'm so glad you found me!" She babbled her thanks and continued hugging us, pressing our three bodies close together. She patted my back with the stump of her arm, ending before the spot where her hands should have been.

"Are you hurt?" Again, not the brightest thing I could have said. But I had to ask her to make sure. She moved as if she was fine, but missing hands was not fine. When we helped her out of the spot where she stood, I saw she was also missing both feet and part of her lower left leg. She did not seem to notice, however, and she positioned herself between the two of us and repeated her gratefulness over and over again until we got her to our cabin.

I could not focus on her litany of words while I worked to clean her wounds. They were jagged and pale, hanging loosely in waterlogged flesh strips. I could not bring myself to remove the strips, and they did not look to be infected. I folded them underneath rags and tied them off.

She finally grew silent and stared at the two of us. She ran one of her stumps along the side of my face, grazing my skin with the newly bound appendage.

"What is your name?"

Before I could answer, my first guest produced a quiet word. "Tabitha."

I had never heard her speak before and was not sure she even could. My emotions warred with the revelation that she had not felt the need to speak to me at all since she had come and yet she found a conversationalist she deemed worthy to answer.

"Thank you for finding me, Tabitha." She turned her attention to me again. "What is your name?" she repeated.

I cleared my throat. "I am called ..." I searched for my desired response. I had a name, surely.

The two of them waited patiently for my response.

"You can call me Fern."

Her eyes became as moist as the air in our room. "Thank you for finding me, Fern."

As I readied us for bed, she finally offered her own moniker. "My name is Jackie."

That night, Tabitha sat in her regular bedtime spot on the edge of the settee. Jackie slept laid out on the short seat tucked behind her.

We found a strong, thick walking stick for Jackie, and she propped it underneath one arm and hobbled about through the swamp with us on our daily treks. Tabitha had retreated back into her mostly silent thoughts, and I was still growing used to having two new companions, so Jackie kept up most of the conversation.

Even she knew how to sit in the silence when we needed to, to listen to what the wind had to tell us.

One day, when the rain sang in thick pounding on the tin roof of our home, an ashen face appeared in the front window of the cabin. Tabitha noticed her and went to open the front door. After what seemed like an eternity, the girl made it inside, dripping with the fresh-scented downpour. I met them with the thickest towels I could find and began to dry her off. She pressed her hands across my face and tangled them in my hair.

"Your hair feels like mine." I glanced at the kinky coils atop her head, sitting regally above black, empty eye sockets that dripped rainwater like pregnant tears.

We led her to the chair in the corner farthest from the fireplace. I did not want her to accidentally move too close to the fire since I was unsure if she could see where she was going.

Jackie, our resident magpie, questioned our newest arrival, barely stopping to wait for the other girl's answers.

Those answers were slow in coming. Her name was Sunny. She did not know how she got there. She was not hurt anywhere. She did not have a preference for where she slept and was happy to simply curl up in the chair. She rested there, the voids of her eyes seeming to stay on alert.

If our family continued to grow, we would need more seats.

The four of us met Naomi when we heard her scream reverberate through the bayou, much shriller and piercing than the cries of the whooping cranes that usually made the most noise. She came crashing through the marsh, headed straight for us, eyes and arms wild and head tilted to the left side.

"Hurry! Run! We have to hide before he comes back for me!" We did not know who she referred to, but we did as she said. She rushed us into the cabin and shut the door soundly, moving furniture to block the door.

"Quick! Close the windows and find something to block them with."

Sunny sat down in her chair.

"Who is coming after you?" I asked as I approached her calmly.

"Him! I didn't think I got away, but after he left me, I ran."

Tabitha joined me behind our new friend. She placed her hands on the place where the girl's neck bent outward in an unnatural angle. The ridge of her vertebrae peeked out in slashes across her skin.

"Hurry ..." Tears fell down her face as she took gulping breaths, and sobs overtook her.

"Are we safe here?" The hope in her eyes could not be hidden, even with the strange way they bulged out of the sockets.

"We are safe here," Sunny responded in her calming, raspy voice.

The newcomer allowed Tabitha and me to lead her to the additional chair that sat near the fireplace. She rubbed her hands together and stared furtively at the blocked door all through the night.

The next day, she told us her name.

"My name is Naomi. Thank you for helping me."

We nodded.

"Y'all seem nice enough and all, but I hate the fucker that brought me here."

I gave her my rapt attention. None of the girls ever talked about their previous lives. I was not the only one interested. Sunny turned her empty eye sockets toward the sound of Naomi's voice. Tabitha's gray, film-covered eye bore into the top of Naomi's tilted head. Jackie rested her chin on the stumps at the end of her arms.

"All I wanted was a drink, dammit. But he wanted so much more from me." She sighed. "I should have known better. I left with him, thinking my blade would keep me safe. It didn't. He broke my neck before he violated me, so there wasn't anything I could do with that old thing."

"What did he look like?" Tabitha's whispery voice floated through the room.

"Big. Tattered blue flannel shirt. Nasty beard."

"Did he drive a beat-up, old, gray pickup truck? That's what the man who left me here dumped me out of after he tied my hands and feet to some rope attached at the back. When he burned off, he took them with him." Jackie waved her stumps around.

"That sounds like him. His back wheel tore this chunk out of my head when he put that nasty thing into reverse. It didn't hurt as much as when he hurt me the other ways …" Tabitha's voice trailed off into nothingness.

All of us looked toward Sunny. She spoke as if she could feel our gazes on her. "I'll never forget how he looked as he scooped my eyes out of my head and spat on me." She knitted her hands together in her lap. "That was him."

We spent the rest of the day in silence, wrapped in our own reveries. I went to bed, consumed by deep sorrow for my sisters of the swamp.

I almost did not hear Naomi when she addressed me the next morning.

"Did he hurt you too?"

I turned to her, sure my confusion showed on my face as she asked me again. I followed her sorrowful gaze to the large gaping opening in my abdomen, the rags of my dress draping down in front of it like the curtain for an opening act.

I had not noticed the wound before. If I had, I just did not remember. I moved my hand around inside, tentatively trying to investigate. I felt the bottom of my ribcage, pulled taut over the remaining tissue that had mummified inside my body. There was no pain, no tenderness. Just nothingness.

I wished the memories had been the same as nothing. I soon remembered bits and pieces of days outside the bayou, days I no longer thought of.

I picked flowers in a meadow. A farmer I vaguely remembered having seen before stopped to speak to me.

"Your mama know you out here by yourself?" He spat a thick stream of spittle directly beside me.

I did not answer him.

He looked around. "You dumb? Can you hear?"

I still did not answer him. There was something off-putting about him, and I did remember feeling scared to take my eyes off him but even more afraid to talk to him.

Instead, I turned to head back toward home. He scooped me up from behind and wrapped his arms around my neck so I could not scream. Something heavy hit me over the head, and darkness came over me.

When I came around again, it was to my entire body aching in places where I should not have had pain. He stooped over me with something in his hands, pounding my torso over and over again. After a while, I stood beside him and watched him defile me in ways I could not prevent, though I screamed and throttled him with my hands and feet.

Finally, he picked me up and put my body in the back of his wagon. I followed on foot until we made it to the edge of my bayou. I stopped when I saw my cabin, deep within the marsh, sunlight glinting off the tin roof. I did not know where he finally placed my body, but I stayed there in the beautiful swamp with the singing trees and whispering wind.

I finally answered Naomi. "No, the one who hurt me is long dead." I looked at each of them with tears in my eyes. "But you just got here. The one who hurt all of you is still out there. And he will be back to bring us more sisters for our cabin."

"Unless we find him." Tabitha's voice startled us in its ferocity, completely different from how we had begun to know her.

I nodded my agreement. We had work to do.

The next few days, we went out around our swamp, scouting. We talked to the birds and listened to the wind to try to determine when he might come back. We had figured out his time schedule but still had to find out where he would come next. He seemed to prefer bringing the girls to the bayou barely alive and then killing them to dump them.

We had not waited long when Jackie heard the rumble of his truck on the north side of the cabin. We ran outside, toward the noise. I arrived first, jumping out in front of his truck as soon as he stopped.

He squinted and stared at me, waving his hand out of his side window. "Get out of the way!"

I was startled that he could see me, but I held my ground. I spread my arms and screamed.

The other girls joined me, surrounding his truck. Muffled grunts met us, and Naomi climbed into the truck bed.

He lumbered out of the driver's seat, glaring at us. "Go on, now. Git! Go mind your business!" He was mostly focused on me as he balled his hands into fists at his sides. Jackie came closer to where I stood, and his eyes widened as he seemed to recognize her.

"What's going on here?" The others closed the circle to surround him. I saw Naomi lead a girl slowly out of the truck and take her to stand with Sunny, who supported her in going to lean on a tree. Then Sunny walked up behind him.

"Y'all can't really be here. I ... I took care of y'all. You ain't really here." He rubbed his eyes.

"You don't believe what you're seeing?" Sunny asked him quietly, her usually dark eye sockets glimmering. "I do. I see the man who killed me."

Naomi added, "The man who killed all of us."

A wet spot appeared in the front of his jeans. Still, he tried to show anger.

"You was askin' for it, all of you! Walkin' around thinkin' you're better than a workin' man. I just wanted to spend a little time with you. You shouldn't have fought me."

"Oh, so we should not fight?" I asked as we drew in closer to him.

"I don't ... I don't know you. Whatever happened to you ain't my problem."

"I know. That does not matter. I will help my sisters here for what you did to them."

I stood directly in front of him and grabbed his arm and took a bite out of it. The other girls jumped on him, biting and stabbing wherever they could. When he was finally rendered motionless, Jackie climbed behind the wheel of his truck and used her limbs to maneuver the truck over his body, again and again, until what remained resembled human mush inside a flannel shirt and jeans full of blood and bits of bone. Then she let the truck roll itself down the incline, where someone would eventually find it.

We all gathered around the girl he left behind.

"How badly did he hurt you?"

"Can you walk?"

She answered in halting words. She was hurt badly, but she was still alive. We could tell because she could not see our wounds.

We walked with her to the edge of the woods surrounding the bayou and stayed with her until a passing car took her to a hospital.

Back at our cabin, we settled in for another night in front of the fire. Soon, despondent yelling broke our solitude.

"Help me!"

I opened the door to see the man we had killed moving only with the rolling gait his condition allowed. Body parts barely pressed together dripped and oozed.

None of us answered him; but the swamp responded. The wind whispered and the trees sang. Gators came up out of the water, and water moccasins followed them. They slithered and ran among the shadows that joined them in devouring his vile spirit, not allowing him respite in our safe haven among the hanging moss.

I hoped there would not be another like him to bring us more sisters. If one came, we would know what to do to save others from spending eternity with us in our little swamp. We, however, would be happy there. Forever.

The River Dog

Blaine Daigle

There's a place in the town where I grew up just over the levee and past the deadfall that separates the risen land and the raging Mississippi River beyond, a small inlet, a swirling pool where lost water from the river's flow pools and lingers like the forgotten memory of a ghost. Technically, it's an extension of the beach that runs longways along the river's curve, the result of dirt and sediment that travels down the beast until it's slung into the corner of the bend. The beach itself is usually a hotspot for all the things normal bored kids in a small town do, gatherings of drunken teenagers who come over the levee on four-wheelers carrying coolers full of beer strapped to the bars. It's where the parties happen. It's where the late-night hookups too scandalous for the watchful gazes of small-town folk happen. The ground is always littered with broken beer bottles or crushed cans, bullet casings from good ole boys shooting into the water, the occasional discarded condom.

But the little inlet? That small swampy area? Nobody goes there.

See, some places are as alive as the people talking about them. Often, those places are haunted, cursed, home to something beyond the scope of the living. This place is all of the above. Stories about this place have been told for God knows how long, and by this point, they've basically become one with the folklore of south Louisiana.

The stories never really match up, though. Some people say the place is the home of something in the low, black water, something with teeth and claws and eyes that glow in the darkness. Some say the ghost of a woman who drowned in the inlet's swirling waters still roams the stretch, her feet never quite touching the ground as she moves endlessly and eternally. But the one that spreads like wildfire throughout the school is that there is a boy there who was abandoned as a baby and raised by alligators. The stories say he still lives in the trees, skulking about in the shallow, swirling water. Watching. Waiting.

That was the story that drove me to going over the levee, the story that pushed me over the deadfall and into the little swamp. It was a dare. I wanted to see the alligator boy. Or even the ghost lady. Maybe I would get a glimpse of whatever those old fishermen said stalked the waters themselves.

What I found ... well, it has never really left me. Even long after I left that town for the last time, with my tail between my legs, it still has its claws in me, so to speak.

I'll warn you upfront—I don't expect you to believe me. There are some nights that I don't know if I believe myself. But I need to say it, get it off my chest. Because if I don't, I don't know what will happen to me.

Just don't expect a kid raised by alligators or a haunted lady. And nothing prowls those waters outside of some big catfish and the occasional gator.

But there was a dog.

I was a kid—a new kid at that. I had only lived in the town for a few months, but even in that brief time, I had become well versed in all the stories. And to a kid like me, a kid raised on *Goosebumps* and *Scooby-Doo*, those stories were too good to pass up. And it wasn't like I had friends to go do things with. Most of my days were spent pining for the life I left behind, hoping beyond hope that I might be able to go back to my old town, my old school. But in the back of my mind, I knew they had already moved on without me. I was stuck, a bored kid who enjoyed things a little on the spooky side. And there it was, something to do.

So I went.

It was a warm Saturday in late September, the final glares of the Louisiana summer beaming down before the brief interlude of fall (if you wanted to even call it that) rolled in and brought the occasional cold front and less-active air conditioners. I didn't have a four-wheeler like everyone else did, and it wasn't like I had people lining up to give me a ride. What I did have was a bike, fresh legs, and a desire to see what all the fuss was about.

By the time I reached the levee, those legs weren't so fresh anymore and a thick sweat sat atop my skin in the afternoon sun. Most of the town's empty spaces were covered in sugarcane fields with rows just wide enough to ride a bike through so long as the ground was hard.

Had it not been for the shortcuts through those fields, I wasn't sure I would have even made it to the levee before dying on the side of the road from a heatstroke.

I sometimes wonder if I would have been better off that way.

Excitement swirled within me as I left my bike at the front of the levee and ascended the slope. I think even then I realized how long it had been since I felt that way, since I felt that rush of adrenaline flood my system and light my nerves on fire.

I don't know if someone would understand unless they've ever been the "new kid," but the town I moved to wasn't the kind of place people left. It was the kind of place people grew up and graduated high school, then left long enough to get a degree before coming back to work in one of the many plants that lined the river parishes of Louisiana. It was a proud community, close-knit and entangled within itself as though the constant renewal of generations overlapped to create something impenetrable, a thicket of family roots too dense to break through.

I felt like an outsider the moment I arrived. Nobody was mean or intentionally disparaging. It just seemed like they all had their own lives already in motion, and I was an outside observer. So I went to the river alone that day.

I climbed the levee and rested a moment atop the gravel trail that ran along its top. On the slope down, the concrete support reached down and ended just as a row of trees began. Beyond that row was the Mississippi River. But even then, I could see the deadfall.

It sat there like a beast all its own. The old and rotting trunks rested atop soft ground, the dead fingers reaching from branches that hadn't seen life in years, maybe decades. There was something forbidding about it, something almost like a threat. It was in the way the trees all lay out so perfectly together that it seemed improbable—no, impossible—for their positioning to be a simple random act of nature.

It was like someone had placed it there, placed them all in such a way that it felt like I was looking at a corpse reaching out to me in a last grasp before death.

I moved slowly toward the deadfall and carefully maneuvered myself around its deceased reach. Occasionally, one of those branches would catch my shirt and pull, and I would have to fight off the instant thought that something was grabbing me. The stories of the boy raised by the alligator flooded my mind, and the sweat on my skin turned cold with the idea.

By the time I got past the deadfall and reached the path on the other side that led to the inlet, the adrenaline had given way to a new feeling—a strange feeling that crept slowly across my bones. Old trees loomed above me like watching figures staring down, choking the sun above and yet providing no real peace in the shade.

It was hard to find peace when a person felt like they were being watched.

But then, after about fifty yards or so, I came across the river. And the inlet.

It looked exactly like I pictured it based on all the stories I had heard. The cypress trees and water oaks that surrounded it drooped over the dirt beach, almost concealing the inlet in shadow. No, even the word inlet didn't make any sense when looking at it. It was the other description now that rang true. Swamp. It felt entirely separate from the river, another organism entirely, without a doubt invisible if viewed from the main course of the river itself. Pools of shallow, dark water filled the lower areas of the beach, dark water I couldn't see into. For the first time, I questioned my own direction. Had I actually found this "beach" or had I accidentally stumbled onto somewhere different? Somewhere darker. Beneath the shade of trees, I felt somehow more alone than I had ever felt before. More than the previous few months of watching everyone around me move on while I stayed still. In that place, that tiny swamp where the water from the raging Mississippi swirled and pulled and lapped against the shores of a dirt beach, I felt as though I was somewhere entirely separated from the world I knew.

Above all else, I remember the quiet. To this day, I remember how I couldn't even hear the river, couldn't hear the swirling waters or the plethora of insects that should have been buzzing about my sweat-laden skin.

I heard nothing except for one sound that, at first, almost slipped by unheard.

The sound of light panting.

I had almost forgotten why I was there in the first place. Suddenly, the stories of swimming monsters and ghost women and alligator-raised kids seemed utterly stupid. I felt myself age, grow up, realize that there were the stupid stories of kids, and then there was *real* danger.

Like being out all alone in a place hidden from the rest of the world.

A place where something was in the brush and panting.

I turned and scanned the area, trying to hone my hearing on where the sound was coming from. As I scanned, I looked for eyes. I looked for a figure in the trees standing at eye level and watching me. I looked for the man I knew had followed me patiently over the levee and around the deadfall. Because that was what it had to be—some vagrant who had seen me so alone on my bike and watched giddily as I moved deeper and deeper into a spider's web.

But there was no man. There were no eyes. There was only the low panting.

Inhale. Exhale. Inhale. Exhale.

For a moment, I wondered if I was just hearing my own rapid breaths, my own beating heart pushing blood through the veins like an engine.

But then my eyes moved down. Down away from the trees along the inlet's edge and toward the thick grass that lined the dirt beach.

To the eyes of the black dog walking out of the grass and onto the beach.

I froze as our gazes met. It was a large dog—not the monstrous form of a Great Dane but rather the size of an adult doberman. The breed, however, was one I hadn't ever seen before. It had the distinctive hind legs of a shepherd, but the long, black fur that covered the rest of its body was almost like a collie. It had a sharp, angular head, with a long snout that tapered down to its pointed noise. Its ears pointed straight in the air, and its black tongue hung from the side of its mouth, rolling over yellow teeth within.

But it was the dog's eyes that struck me deepest. At first glance, they seemed brown, the same kind of deep brown that any of the lovable companions I had back home might well have had. The more I looked, however, the more I realized they weren't brown. What I was seeing was simply a reflection of the muddy water that swirled behind me.

The dog's eyes were black.

Instinctively, I took a step back. The dog, in turn,

stepped forward out of the tall grass. Its tongue rolled with each heavy pant, and as it moved with me, I swore I saw something in its face. Something that made my blood run cold beneath my skin.

It was smiling.

"Hey, boy," I said, my voice shaking with every syllable. "What are you doing out here?"

The dog turned its head slightly, and its tongue hung limply. Its ears perked with the sound of my voice, and for a moment of what I assumed at that moment was insanity, I wondered if it understood me.

Then it stepped forward again.

I responded with another step back, stopping only when I felt the lapping water soak my shoes as I reached the bank. The smile I thought I saw before was apparent, painted upon the animal's face, the back of its mouth turning up toward its eyes.

Those black eyes stayed locked on my own. It took another step toward me, but I didn't respond. I couldn't. The churning water where the Mississippi River poured into the swamp was at my back and atop my feet, soaking my shoes and socks.

It stepped again.

Alone became a word that held more meaning than it ever had before.

"Go!" I screamed at the dog. "Go on! Get away!"

But the dog didn't move. It didn't even stop smiling. There was something sinister in that smile, something dark and corrupt within those eyes.

For a moment, I felt my own trembling legs give way to … was it comfort? Contentment? There I was, facing man's best friend.

I didn't have a best friend. I didn't even have a single friend. All the ones I had before had moved on from me. They probably already forgot who I was. Someone would say my name, and they would reply, "Wait, who is that?" Then they would realize their mistake and say, "Oh yeah, I forgot about him." After that, they would slip right back into forgetting, right back into the lives that moved on without me.

Maybe the dog was something more. Maybe it was rabid. Maybe it would leap and tear at my throat and leave me choking in my own blood miles away from anyone who would hear me.

But was it so different from where I already was?

I snapped out of the trance and felt the fear return. The dog was closer. Closer. Ever closer with each slow step across the dirt beach.

I reached down into the water and felt for something hard, something I could hold in my hand. When my hand moved over the smooth surface of a baseball-sized rock, adrenaline surged within me.

"Get back!" I yelled.

But the dog didn't listen. It stepped again, smiling all the while.

I reached back and threw the rock as hard as I could. The dog was only a few yards away and my aim was good. The rock hit the animal square in its long snout. For a moment, it recoiled. But it didn't yelp, didn't run.

Instead, the animal turned back to me. Its eyes blazed with fury, and that horrid smile grew wider. Those yellow teeth bared their entire lengths. That black tongue dripped with saliva. I realized then that the animal wasn't panting. It was salivating.

In a fluid motion, the dog rose to its hind legs, raising its head higher than my own. Its front shoulders contorted slightly, almost like squaring off, and its paws rose to its elevated chest. At their ends were long, black claws that curved downward like sickles. That awful smile opened up. Those eyes burned even more ferociously, and the animal let out a cackling sound. There was no echo. It sounded like laughter—a deep, unhinged, maniacal laughter.

The dog ran at me. It covered the space in a fraction of a second, and my only recourse was to duck and roll. I felt the claws hit my shoulder, the impact accompanied by a popping sensation of being punctured. I ducked low enough that most of the animal went tumbling over me, the claws in my shoulder raking across my shoulder blades and down to my lower back. A searing pain erupted from the lacerations, but the adrenaline in my system kept me going. We fell into the water, and the animal continued its roll, the claws leaving my skin as it tumbled farther into the inlet pool.

I struggled to my feet. The warm waters of the Mississippi blended with the warmer flow of blood running down my back. A few steps later and my feet hit the hard dirt, the sudden traction propelling me forward so quickly I stumbled and fell. As I rose to my feet, I looked behind me to see the dog rising from the water and turning that baleful glare back to me.

I ran.

I ran as hard as I could. I didn't know if I heard footsteps behind me. I didn't know if the dog was chasing me on two legs or four. I didn't know if it followed me and, if it did, where it finally stopped.

All I know, and all I remember, is that horrible laugh, the cackle bouncing off the trees as I ran back to the levee, back to the deadfall that held no doubt in my mind about the purpose of its construction. It was a barrier, a warning, an obstacle laid by someone who had stumbled across the same thing I did. Who had seen the river dog and gotten away.

I surged up and over the levee, losing my footing on the other side and rolling down to the ditch where my bike lay. Then I rode. I pedaled as hard as I could for as long as I could, cutting through the sugarcane fields and praying the entire time that the ground wouldn't soften beneath my tires.

The whole way back, I heard that laughter. It was in my head, I think, but God, it sounded like it was right at my back the entire way.

By the time I got home, my legs were numb and dead and there wasn't a square inch of me uncovered by sweat. I leaped off the bike and threw it to the side before I had even stopped and exploded through the front door of my house, slamming it behind me and throwing every lock and deadbolt into place. Then I collapsed to the floor and let my breathing slow.

The smaller my breaths got, the more the tears ran down my face.

I told my parents, and everyone else who asked, that I had been attacked by a dog. It seemed truthful enough without raising obvious questions about my sanity. They responded with a heap of bandages and the miserable experience of rabies shots. I didn't tell them where I was. I just said I had been out in the cane fields. That little inlet didn't need to be disturbed. That deadfall was evidence enough it was a place home to something else, something we weren't meant to coexist with.

I never told a soul what happened to me on that day. But it always came back in my dreams. Dreams where I relived the experience of that day over. And over. And over. And over again. It was as if it was refusing to let me forget, refusing to let me let go and move on.

But like most things, memories fade after a while. Time moved on, and the rigors of everyday life as the new kid eventually consumed me. I barely had time to think about anything, and that was ok. If it meant I would never see those eyes and that smile ever again, then so be it.

I made a few friends, integrated myself as best I could into the society of school. I played sports, fully realizing that the time was coming quickly when I would no longer be able to, when whatever potential I had would peak and simply not be enough anymore. I went to a few of the local festivals around town, tried my best to make myself at least exist on the outer rings of that tangled web of roots.

But a year to the day after I had gone around that deadfall and walked into that swamp, the river dog came back.

It was a warm night, just like that day had been. I woke in the middle of the night to a scratching at my window. At first, I figured a breeze had come through and was pushing the branches of the oak tree outside my window. Because that was what it always was, right? In all the horror movies, it was the tree, wasn't it?

It wasn't the tree that time.

Beneath the window, I looked up to see a horrifically familiar silhouette on the other side. Backlit by a full moon, the dark outline of that long snout angled down. Down to me.

A soft cackle filled the room.

I pulled the covers over my head as my heart broke into a sprint. *It's not real,* I told myself. *It's not real.*

But was it? I hadn't looked behind me the whole way home that day. How far had it followed me, really? How many times could it have taken me but instead decided to let me go, choosing instead to follow and observe? To see where I lived so one day, when it was hungry enough, it would return to where it knew the pantry was stacked.

I peeked out from the covers to see that dark claw fiddling with the locked latch, trying to pop it open and slide the window up. I pulled the covers back over me. For hours I listened to that soft laughter and the steady ticking of that claw prying at the window. But it never got in. When the sun finally rose, the beast was gone.

I waited in dreadful anticipation for the next night, knowing it would show again.

But it didn't.

Not for another year.

And the year after that.

And after that.

Every year. The same night. The beast at my window, itching to get in. Laughing at me while I hid, crying beneath the covers like a child.

The moment I turned eighteen, I left. College and the promise of a new future far from that town and that inlet and my yearly visitor was calling. The last time I left that place, I made sure to drive out by the levee, going up the lone trail to the top to ensure the deadfall was still there. When I saw that it was, I put the truck in drive and rolled away, swearing never to return.

Over the next four years, I went through the same process of feeling like the new kid again. The friends I managed to make in high school had gone off on their own adventures, scattering to different parts of the state and country. We kept in touch for a while, but like before, everyone's life moved on. I didn't move with them. So in a new place with new people, I began the process once again.

But on that night, that same night every year, I made sure I was not alone in my dorm. I was at a bar, a party I heard about even if I hadn't been officially invited. I made sure I was around as many people as possible. But despite the safety that crowds brought, there was always that feeling of emptiness, as though I was surrounded by moving pictures painted in unfamiliar colors. I felt like a bookmark, a placeholder, putting myself into those situations for literal safekeeping.

Life moved around me, and I watched it disappear in the distance. I watched the connections I made dissolve with the passing days, months, and years. I realized that the people I had known were little more than ghosts, remnants of who they were before, the vapors of the day dissipated by sleep and then relegated to memory by the arrival of the morning.

I wanted to leave my ghosts behind as well, yet I found myself haunted by the person who refused to fade away. Who refused to give up the ghost. The person who still heard that manic laugh and saw that horrific smile. Who still felt the stare of those eyes. I felt as though I had left that place cursed to walk forever and yet get nowhere, the constant strain of starting anew an exhaustive punishment for my sin of ignoring the deadfall.

I graduated and got a job. I bought a house, a small home in serious need of updates and renovations that sat on five acres of lightly wooded land. I picked that place for a reason. It was isolated. It was peaceful. It was far from the reminders that everyone I knew had moved on without me.

Then the dog came back.

I stayed in for the first time in years. Why? I couldn't tell you even today. But I fell asleep on the front porch. When I woke up, I looked across the field that led to the trees at the edge of the property.

The dog was there, standing upright, the silhouette of its shoulders unnaturally squared off. The soft panting carried across the property somehow, the only sound in the night.

I ran back inside and locked the doors. When I went to the window, it was gone. For a moment, I thought it was in my head. For a moment, I thought maybe I actually imagined it all. That the memory of that day at the inlet past the deadfall was nothing more than the machinations of a lonely mind.

But that night, I woke to see the beast at my window. Backlit by the moonlight, It fumbled at the window latch.

Laughing. Giggling. Taunting me.

It has been that way for years now. It returns every year, but I've stopped running. Somehow, the dog's constant and consistent intrusion is more than I ever got from any of my other relationships.

God help me, I started to think of the beast as the one constant in my life. It was the one thing that hadn't left me. While everyone else moved on, the dog stayed. While everyone else became the ghosts of memory, the dog lingered in the present. Reliable. Consistent. Man's best friend.

My best friend.

The fact that those thoughts went through my head,

still go through, terrifies me. Unnerves me. Shakes the deepest part of my soul with untamed vigor.

And yet, tonight, I'm going to leave the latch unlocked. Tonight, some sick part of me hopes the river dog will return, that it won't leave like everyone else did. Because anything is better than this constant loneliness.

Tonight, I'll wait for my old friend to come home.

The Heart of Gaia

Red Lagoe

Simon Dartmouth sat in first class as coach passengers shuffled by. His heart pounded with the unremitting thrill of conquest. As soon as the artifact was in his possession earlier that day, he paddled out of the bayou, back to his hotel for his belongings, and caught the first flight to New York.

Beneath his shirt, a thin copper wire cradled the palm-sized stone that hung from a black pendant cord around his neck. He placed his hand on his chest against his treasure, silently reveling in the most significant moment of his career when his phone buzzed.

He answered the call from his colleague, Daniel, with a simple, "I got it."

"Are you serious?" Daniel gasped. "I can't believe she let it go."

"You'd be surprised what people would give up for the right price."

"So, she took the offer?" Daniel asked.

"Well, I'm out five hundred thousand, so ..."

The flight attendant took her position in the middle of the aisle to begin the preflight safety spiel.

"We're taking off. I'll see you tomorrow morning." Simon closed the conversation and massaged the stone under his shirt. He had finally done it. The Heart of Gaia was in his possession. Power and wealth beyond his imagination was within his grasp. The mystical energy of the stone seemed to already surge through him, or perhaps that was the lingering intoxication of adventure.

As the galvanic sensation coursed through his blood, he wondered if the people around him could sense his success. Maybe the doe-eyed flight attendant at the front could smell its power on him like alpha pheromones. She locked eyes and suggestively blew into the flotation device nozzle during her demonstration. She could be his second treasure—a bonus prize—to acquire on his trip. But Simon had to focus on getting the stone back to New York for assessment.

As his eyes traversed her body, the irritating whine of a mosquito buzzed around his head. He swatted at the insect, but it persisted, swooping in and out of earshot.

The plane climbed higher, and as clouds floated beneath him, he was reminded of the reflection of clouds in the gentle, flowing waters of the bayou. He had rented a kayak to make the last leg of his trip to the old woman's boathouse, using a hand drawn map provided by a local fisherman for a mere hundred bucks. Cypress trees had towered overhead. Their knees—the knobby roots that would otherwise suffocate beneath the decaying swamp floor—rose above the waterline at the base of the tree like tiny cloaked figures. Spanish moss hung deadly still in the stagnant air. The humidity was as thick as soup, and sweat drenched his clothing. No matter how much DEET he sprayed, incessant mosquitoes swarmed and bit at his flesh.

A high-pitched ringing in his ear broke him from his memory, bringing him back to his first-class seat. A sharp sting drew his attention to his hand, where a mosquito had burrowed its proboscis deep into a protruding vein. Simon tensed, then smacked it, popping its body and splattering freshly siphoned blood across the back of his hand.

After his flight and taxi, Simon rolled his luggage to the entrance of his Manhattan building. The doorman smiled as he entered, and his building manager, Henrietta, gave him a smirk and a "Welcome back."

The elevator opened on the thirtieth floor, and he unlocked his apartment door. Orange light from the setting sun flooded the apartment through floor-to-ceiling windows. The artificial lights of the city skyline began to glow, and Simon stepped out of his sunken living room up three steps to his bedroom, where he hoisted his suitcase onto the bed and opened the zipper.

As the luggage peeled open, a massive insect the size of his hand flew out of the bag and onto the floor. In the south, they called them waterbugs, but to Simon, they were exactly what they looked like—oversized cockroaches. He chased after it, stomping with each step, trying to smash the thing under his boot. The insect made it halfway across his bedroom before he finally caught it. The stowaway's guts burst through its ruptured exoskeleton and clung to Simon's boot tread.

It sickened him that he brought part of the old woman's deplorable boathouse back with him, because that meant the little critter must have been on his body when he left. He shivered at the thought but quickly dismissed his disgust. A minor infestation would be worth it considering the treasure he carried.

He had chased the artifact for over a decade. The Heart of Gaia was an obscure treasure, rumored to be a myth and dismissed by the archaeological community. Its roots began in ancient Egypt, then to Mesopotamia, into Europe, and eventually the coasts of Louisiana via the ship of the famed Pirate Lafitte. Simon and his colleague, Daniel, had followed the carvings, the letters, the stories, and a broken line of ancestry to an old woman whose last address was in Lafayette, Louisiana. The Heart of Gaia (if all their research was correct) would bring its steward prosperity and abundance, and there was ample historical evidence to prove it worked, aside from a few holes in its history. Tomorrow, Simon would meet with Daniel, who would help him fill in those holes and unravel the mechanics of its mystical properties.

He removed his jacket and shirt and stood in the sun's failing light to admire the colors in the stone. Everything had happened so fast in Louisiana, Simon hadn't taken the time to truly admire it. Layers appeared to swirl like the algae and the natural oils of decay on the waters of the bayou. Greens and blues curled into pale yellow, all circling a center as black as obsidian. His reflection in the stone's center ebbed and flowed with his breaths, pulsing with the swirling motion of the pendant's stone.

Simon's reflection grew larger as he leaned in for a closer look. As he drew near, his eye filled the black midsection. His lid rolled back from the protruding eye as if it was about to rupture from its socket.

He startled into reality, and the stone's reflective qualities receded with the failing daylight. *You are not the steward*, the old woman had said. Ancient, knowing eyes withheld the stone's secrets—secrets she had no right keeping for herself.

The vision of the bulging eye in the stone was no more than exhaustion taking its toll. He needed rest, and his aching body desperately needed a shower to remove the stench of the swamp. Unable to risk parting with the stone, even if only by a few feet, he left it hanging from his neck while he stepped under the cascading water of his shower. It rained over his face, reminding him of the dense humidity and curtains of Spanish moss that he had bushwacked out of his path as the bayou's twists and turns had become narrower.

The old woman's boathouse seemed to appear out of nowhere. It was a surprise to Simon that the old vessel was still afloat considering the surrounding vegetation had grown into its walls. The swamp was devouring the woman's home, and if he didn't get the stone out of there, it would be lost forever.

She was a stubborn old hag, and by the looks of her shelves full of suspicious jars, hanging dried leaves, and random sticks and crystals, he suspected she was a witch. Her eyes, now that he had time to think about it, reminded him of the colors of the stone. They were green and blue, with streaks of brown, yellow, and black. She had told him in a thick Cajun accent that sounded more French than it did anything else, "It must stay here. It is linked to the bayou and catastrophic for anyone who removes it."

"Well now, I know that isn't true, ma'am," he had said with a smile. "The stone was once linked to Egypt, and then to France. So, I know for a fact that it'll work wherever it goes."

She squinted her eyes. "Sonny, you don't understand Gaia, do you now?"

"I understand that the stone you've got there around your neck has brought 'prosperity to all who carry it.'" Simon quoted the ancient tablet and scanned the ramshackle interior of her home. "Doesn't look like it's working so good for you, so I'm willing to offer you a deal." He set a black backpack on the table beside her.

The old woman with thin gray hair didn't even glance at the bag. "Do you know how important the wetlands are to the earth? Do you know what would happen if the stone was not here anymore? The stone goes to where it is needed."

"The swamp will be fine, ma'am. I promise." He gestured to her walls. Vines had invaded years ago, climbing across the ceiling, and moss and mildew covered the floors. "But I can't say the same for this place."

Simon unzipped the backpack to expose stacks of bills. It may as well have glowed like golden sunlight, it was such a beautiful sight.

The old woman clutched the pendant and took a step back. "No, thank you. The stone stays here, where it belongs."

"I'm giving you the opportunity of a lifetime ... half a million dollars, ma'am. Think about that for a minute."

The old woman straightened her posture and held her

chin up. "You can leave now."

Simon's smile faded and twisted into a sneer. "I'm not going anywhere without that stone."

She spit on the floor at his feet, and the boathouse filled with the stench of the swamp, reeking of rotten wood and decay.

Even at that moment, as he stood in his pristine New York City apartment under clean water, he could smell the acrid aroma of the bayou's lesser-traveled stagnant waterways.

Simon dried off, brushed his teeth, and slid his aching body under silk sheets. His shoulders screamed from the full day of paddling.

The old woman would not allow him to rest, though. She came to him in his dream. She stood before his bag of money and spit on his offer. "You cannot decide where it goes. Only Gaia can."

He wasn't going to change her mind with negotiation. But after a decade of research and dozens of overseas excavations, how could he have left empty handed? The old witch had no right keeping it for herself after all those years, not even bothering to use it. He wrapped his hands around her neck, threatening to kill her, but she was not deterred. She gripped the stone tighter, raised it to her lips, and whispered into it. Her voice was raspy and unintelligible.

"Yes, say goodbye to it," he had said, ready to release her.

But instead of letting go, giving into his threat, she lifted her eyes to his and laughed. "The stone is not done here. Gaia refuses you."

Simon's tempered rage boiled beyond his control. His gentle yet threatening grip on her neck tightened. Crepe-paper skin wrinkled and shifted beneath his palms. Her pale flesh immediately bruised into yellows and purples flushing to the surface as he crushed blood vessels. The old woman's eyes widened as the pressure in her head increased. Her eyeballs pressed against her lids, bulging near out of her skull. Pink conjunctiva protruded and vessels burst, spilling blood that inked across white sclera. Her gaze never left him as her body went limp. The full weight of her frail existence was hardly a struggle to hold up with one hand.

Simon released her neck, and she collapsed to the damp floorboards in a heap. Eyes swollen in their sockets continued to stare into him with warning, and her fingers maintained a death grip upon her amulet.

Simon startled awake with a jerk. The dream was an exact recall of the events that had transpired the day before. His hand was clutched around the stone on his chest as he remembered prying her dead fingers away from it. Her bones had snapped as he wrenched her fingers back to get to the Heart of Gaia.

Sweat had soaked through his T-shirt and silk sheets. His hairline was drenched and overflowing down his forehead and into his eyes.

He lifted the pendant from his chest and gazed into the black abyss at the stone's center, questioning his actions. Perhaps he should have listened to the old woman before breaking it from her hands. He had worked with enough cursed objects to know better. Her haunting voice played in his head: *Gaia refuses you.*

There was no time to worry about the past. What was done was done, and Daniel was key to discovering the true powers behind it. If there was a curse, he would help remove it.

Simon swung his feet over the edge of the bed, using his forearm to wipe away sweat, but his entire body was covered. He hit the switch on his curtains, and as they glided open, they did not reveal the stunning view of the skyline at dawn, but rather a thick layer of condensation on the inside of the glass.

A stifling, thick heat filled his apartment as he shuffled toward the bedroom door. Slick, wet feet navigated the three steps down into the living room, nearly slipping in his own sweat. However, as he reached the plush area rug near the thermostat, he realized sweaty feet were not the problem. His entire floor was damp. The carpet squished underfoot, water oozing out of the fibers into a small puddle around his toes. The thermostat was set right where it needed to be at seventy-two degrees, but he lowered the temperature anyway to sixty-five to offset whatever was going on. On any other day, he would've immediately called the building manager, Henrietta, to send maintenance, but there was too much to do. His priority was getting the pendant to Daniel for assessment.

Simon arrived at the little metaphysical shop in Tribeca, and Daniel flipped the door sign to closed, rubbing his hands together. The scrawny man was clean-shaven and smelled like sandalwood. He gestured for Simon to head toward the back of the shop. They ushered by shelves of artifacts, oddities, crystals, and items of the occult.

Daniel's workshop was in the back. He specialized

in rare, supernatural objects, and a few years earlier, he had tried to help Simon uncover the subtle magical properties of a sarcophagus he had acquired on the black market. The sarcophagus proved fairly useless when Daniel discovered that the person entombed had been a simple farmer.

Simon, already sweating from the trip over, stepped up to Daniel's work bench and set the stone under the lamp. "What's your first impression? Is this it? Is this what I've been looking for?"

Daniel's jaw dropped at the sight. Using a jeweler's loupe to inspect it, he leaned in. "I see maybe labradorite. Is that lapis lazuli? Amazonite? Obsidian center.... Fits the description, I'd say."

Simon nodded as he observed, waiting for Daniel to do his thing and feel out its real powers. Any archaeologist or appraisal specialist could tell him the composition and if the stone was authentic, but Daniel had a special ability to sense the history of an object. It was how he had known the sarcophagus had an entombed farmer instead of a pharaoh.

Daniel shook out his arms. "This might take a while. You can go grab a coffee or whatever."

"I'm not going anywhere."

Daniel sighed, eyebrows climbing his forehead. "Okay. But be quiet. I need to focus."

Simon moved to an opposite corner in the room while Daniel relaxed his shoulders, cupped his hands in a bubble around the amulet, and stared directly into the stone.

Simon eased into a cushioned chair in the corner among random artifacts and collectibles. Gemstones and crystals sat neatly on shelves, backlit by blue light. There were samurai swords and a dagger with a dragonhead handle on display. A replica of Galileo's telescope stood in the corner.

Before Simon could cross his leg over his knee and get comfortable, Daniel's stool scraped the tile floor and he stepped away from the amulet. "What did you do?" Daniel asked, mouth hanging open. His eyes pierced into Simon's soul with judgment.

"What did you *see*?" Simon asked.

"I think you know. And now I'm asking you, *what did you do?*" His jaw rippled as he clenched his teeth.

"What I had to," Simon snarled, raising from his seat.

"You strangled her?" Daniel placed a hand against his heart.

Simon approached him, took a steadying breath to compose himself rather than grabbing Daniel by the collar to shake him down. "This kind of artifact can't lay in the hands of some swamp witch for all eternity."

"Is she dead?"

He fought the urge to lash out. "I asked you to tell me how it works, not to spy on me with your psychic abilities."

"I don't pick what I see," Daniel said. "You said she took the money."

"That's not exactly what I said, now, is it? Leaving the money is an anonymous hush offer for whoever finds her body."

"What the hell is going on, Simon? I didn't sign up for this."

"This is exactly what you signed up for!" Simon charged toward him, and the skinny man staggered a step backward. The pressure in his skull climbed. His veins throbbed in his neck. "Sit your ass down and tell me how this thing works or they'll be hauling your fucking corpse out of this place!"

Daniel shook his head, eyes going glassy. "Fine. Leave it with me for a couple days and I'll see what I can figure out."

Simon grabbed a dragonhead handled blade from the display rack as Daniel fell over his stool, trembling. Simon dove to the ground and held the blade to his throat. "You'll do it now."

Teeth chattering, Daniel regained his upright posture after being released. A stiff chin fought the trembling as he slid his stool up to his workbench and sat before the stone.

"It doesn't have to be this complicated!" Simon wiped sweat from his brow and hung his jacket over the back of the chair in the corner, heart galloping with fury as he tried to simmer the rage.

Once Daniel stopped shaking, he became very still at his bench. A trance-like state fell over him, and his body swayed gently forward and backward, eyes peeled open, unblinking into the ancient stone.

Simon watched on edge, waiting for something magical to happen—a portal to open, an ancient deity or jinn to come spilling out of the stone in a black cloud, or perhaps a light would shoot out of it across the room. However, only silence pervaded, and the sticky stench of the swamp filled his nostrils.

After about half an hour, Daniel pulled away from the stone and stretched.

"What?" Simon asked.

"I don't think it's what we thought it was."

"All the evidence says otherwise."

"Right. But there were gaps that we filled in with speculation. I think we were wrong."

"How so?"

"I saw ... farmers getting the rain they needed,

relieving a drought. I saw the Nile and a bountiful harvest on its shores. I saw a forest in France thriving, teeming with life. I got the word *ecosystem*."

"So, what is all that supposed to mean?"

"This stone isn't to make people wealthy. It's to make the ecosystem healthy."

"What the fuck are you telling me? *Abundance and prosperity!* Those were the messages. Every person who owned this stone was insanely rich." Simon's teeth ground together, fearing Daniel was lying.

Daniel's brow furrowed and he chewed his lip. "Maybe the prosperity was because the land they lived on was abundant.... It's so obvious!" Daniel shook his head, body slumping in disappointment. "Heart of Gaia is the heart of the earth. What the earth wants."

Simon paced the floor. "The old woman said Gaia chooses. The Heart has been all over the world. Someone decides to take it to the next place. Who decides that? This thing would've been buried under six feet of swamp water in a year if I didn't acquire it. Maybe *Gaia* wants me to have it. That's why I found it."

They both looked to the stone beneath the work lamp. The colors seemed to glow under the light, its black center a void as dark as a black hole.

Simon ran his fingers along the outer edges. "Yes. I am its new steward, so how do I make it work for me? How do I let it help *my* environment? The urban jungle.... Wall Street.... Different times call for different rules."

Daniel's face twitched subtly, but enough for Simon to know that he didn't approve. He shrugged. "Maybe whoever has the stone has to charge it with new magic to make it improve the natural surroundings of its new home. That's the way other magical objects tend to work."

"Well how the hell would they do that?"

"It's sort of like reprogramming a crystal for magic. Maybe it needs to sit in the sun, or the full moon's light. Maybe it requires a cleansing or some sort of ritual magic. I'll have to review the texts again to see if there's something we missed, but I honestly don't think this thing is going to make you rich. I'm sorry. But it's the farmer in the sarcophagus all over again."

"I'll decide whether or not it'll make me rich." Simon grabbed it from the table. He hung it from his neck as he headed toward the storefront. The amulet was so heavy against his chest it felt like it could bore a hole clear through his flesh. "We're done here."

Daniel followed at his heels. "Ancient civilizations relied a lot on the natural world and its mystical properties. It's not unheard of that someone may have found this stone—or forged it—with the intent of using it as a tool to protect their lands. That's all it does!"

"Then I'll make it work in my favor. My environment is here, and it's just as important to me as the fucking bayou was to that crazy old swamp witch. I *will* wield this power to my benefit one way or another." He opened the front door to the shop, and the bell jingled.

"Spells and curses and witchcraft can be created for any purpose, but the universe has a way of balancing out what's good and bad for the laws of nature," Daniel said as Simon exited. "You can't *trick* these kinds of things!" Daniel shouted after him.

Simon didn't look back. He may not have been able to trick the universe, but he could trick a fucking rock.

When he arrived home, drenched in sweat, the walls were still damp and fog clung to the windows. The pervasive stench of swamp water bled through his clothes and soaked into his hair. A thin film of green coated the coffee table, and a roachlike bug skittered across the floor and disappeared under the couch. The air was so dense with moisture it was difficult to inhale fully.

It was clear to him that the pendant around his neck was responsible for it. Simon removed his clothes and stepped into a cool shower to relieve the heat and contemplate his next move. On the walls in his bathroom, a green slime had begun to form on the tiles.

The Heart of Gaia worked, but it was still linked to the bayou. It was simply a matter of figuring out its underlying code—the conditions or rituals needed to reprogram the thing to his benefit. If The Heart of Gaia protected the environment in which it was programmed, then he could make it work to his financial benefit. Hell, he could use it to terraform a desert into a tropical oasis and build a realty empire around it.

Simon stepped under the water, studying the amulet as the colors swirled and swelled with each of his breaths. His eyes relaxed, trying to feel its power, trying to connect with it on some metaphysical plane—to become its steward. The black center expanded like a pupil on LSD, and within the darkness, he could see the old woman dead on the floor of her boathouse. Beyond her, a snake slithered out the door and into the algae-coated swamp water. Cypress trees were towers in the water, creating a canopy of leaves and Spanish moss overhead.

He wasn't sure when the shower water had turned warm, but it was as if he woke from his trance under the torrential rain of a Louisiana afternoon storm. He cut the water to the shower, and algae smeared onto his palm from the knob. Above, long tendrils of Spanish moss grew from the ceiling. The sight made him laugh in amazement, and he scrambled for the shower door, tripping over a Cypress root on the way out. The glass door flung open, and he spilled out of the shower into thick sludge covering the floor. The knobby roots of the Bald Cypress tree had grown out of his shower floor and broke through the grout in the tiles across his bathroom.

Simon didn't know if he should be afraid or inspired by the reality of the stone's magic.

He held the stone to his lips with tears in his eyes, then whispered into it the way the old swamp witch had done right before he strangled her. "You will not refuse me."

He peeled himself from the swampy sludge, rising to his feet. As he made his demands to Gaia, a sharp bite at his ankle caused him to scream out. A coral snake, red, black, and yellow, slithered away behind the toilet. The venomous creature left a welt on his ankle, and capillaries at the surface of his skin turned black at the bite wound. Simon staggered haphazardly out of the bathroom and into a transformed apartment.

Moss hung like curtains from above. Mosquitoes swarmed his bare skin, and he swatted to keep them from landing. His attention drawn to the canopy of green on his ceiling, he failed to notice the pool of swamp water that had filled his recessed living room. His body plunged waist deep, breaking a layer of algae on the surface. His feet sank into the sticky, decaying muck of the swamp floor. Like quicksand, the harder he pulled, the deeper he sank. Simon traversed the living room slowly, sinking farther each time he yanked his foot from the soft floor. Chest deep, he grabbed his cellphone from the floating coffee table to call for help, but it had sat in a puddle of moisture and would not turn on.

The setting sun's light broke through condensation streaks in the window and lit the surface of the water sideways, turning the oily slick of natural decay into a rainbow of colors matching those of the amulet. Captivated by the swirling hues, he had difficulty pulling himself from its beauty, but he had to get back to Daniel with this new development.

But the spongey floor pulled him deeper with each step toward the door. Simon kept one hand clutched around the stone, raising it above the water, and continued across his apartment. Ears submerged, his chin raised skyward as the swamp pulled him farther into its deadly grip. Above, the white ceiling and recessed lighting was lost to the canopy of Cypress and moss. Peat moss and decay at the swamp floor ensnared him. One more attempt at a step pulled him under. Dark black water filled his mouth. Rot and algae coated his teeth. He spit it out, but there was nowhere for it to go but back into his body.

Instinctively, he coughed and pulled in a gasp, but all that came was the dank, stagnant water flooding his lungs. The sharp stabbing pain in his chest became a dull, quiet ache. His eyes went under and his world turned to black, then a lush green. The sound of the bayou's whispering trees and the trickle of a paddle in the water came to him. The sickly sweet stench of death and decay reminded him of the cycle of life. Simon's oxygen-deprived brain allowed him a moment of respite. His muscles stopped fighting. His head ceased thrashing from side to side, and his fingers released their grip from The Heart of Gaia.

Daniel hadn't heard from Simon in a few days and didn't care to ever see him again. He should've stopped working with that man years ago, but the job was so exciting he had difficulty pulling away. He had always known there was a sinister side to Simon, but it never revealed itself until he killed that woman.

Daniel had wiped his hands clean of the incident until a dream came to him last night. The message was clear: the stone was without a steward and needed to get back to its biome. Maybe that was how he could make right of the situation and relieve himself of the guilt of the old woman's death.

Simon's calls went unanswered, so Daniel showed up at his building. The doorman wouldn't allow him in without permission from Simon, but he allowed him to express his concerns with the building manager, Henrietta. She was a sturdy woman with copper skin and a kind heart. Her good intentions practically glowed in an aura around her, and after a few minutes, they were at Simon's door on the thirtieth floor.

"Mr. Dartmouth?" Henrietta said, knocking on the door. She turned the key and knocked again. Daniel stood behind her, fairly certain of what he was about to see.

She cracked the door, and a waft of pungent air hit Daniel in the face.

Henrietta turned her head and gagged. "Mr. Dartmouth?" She pushed the door open fully.

Simon's body lay only a few feet from the door and was unrecognizable. It had bloated double his size as if it had been submerged at the bottom of a lake for the past few days. The room was damp and covered in algae, and he lay naked and decaying on the floor while massive, black water bugs scattered from their feast on his body. His skin was marbled blue, green, yellow, and necrotic black. Around his neck was the pendant.

Henrietta screamed, and Daniel forged a shocked expression while she ran down the hall. While she stood by the elevators, calling 911, Daniel stepped closer to Simon's body, then glanced over his shoulder to be sure Henrietta wasn't looking.

He peeled the pendant from Simon's flesh. The black cord stuck to his rotten skin, and bits of Simon came off as Daniel stripped it away. He pocketed the amulet, then hurried to the elevator feeling like he might vomit. He ran from the scene, faking tears and hysteria so Henrietta wouldn't suspect he had taken anything.

Daniel hurried to the nearest Metro station and jumped on a train. The stone reeked of death, and he wondered if everyone could smell it on him. He clutched it in his palm, under his shirt, feeling the stone's energy. It wanted to return to the bayou, and originally, that was his plan. But since he had seen first person what it could do, perhaps Simon was onto something. Perhaps it could be used in another environment. If anyone could recharge or reprogram The Heart of Gaia, it would be Daniel, after all.

As he schemed a way to control its power, the sickly stench of decay lingered in his nose. The algae film from Simon's apartment had gotten on his pants. Then there was a high pitched ringing in his ear—no, not ringing. A buzz. He waved his hand at his ear and shooed away the threatening whine of a mosquito.

Publisher's Note

Thank you for reading Screams From The Bayou. This anthology wouldn't exist without you, the reader.

If you enjoyed this book, please consider leaving a review on Amazon, GoodReads, or your favorite social media platform.

Please visit our website for more information about our releases and signed copies of our books.
www.brokenbrainbooks.com

Other Anthologies by Broken Brain Books
Screams From Outer Space
Screams From The Ocean Floor
Screams From Beyond The Veil
Screams From The Dark Ages
Books of Horror Indie Brawl Anthology

Also available
Usher of the Fallen by LM Kaplin
We All Fall Before The Harvest by C.M. Forest
Rorschach by Aaron Lebold
Mine by LM Kaplin
Fang Fiction by LM Kaplin
Ruby's Cube by Lyla Diamond
Pacheco Pass by Aaron Lebold

About the Authors

Jonathan Janz

Jonathan Janz is an author and public schoolteacher. His sci-fi horror novel VEIL is now available, and you can find his story "Lenora" in THE END OF THE WORLD AS WE KNOW IT: NEW TALES OF STEPHEN KING'S THE STAND. He's represented for Film & TV by Adam Kolbrenner of Lit Entertainment, and his literary agent is Lane Heymont. His ghost story The Siren and the Specter was selected as a Goodreads Choice nominee for Best Horror. Additionally, his novels Children of the Dark and The Dark Game were chosen by Booklist and Library Journal as Top Ten Horror Books of the Year. Jonathan's main interests are his wonderful wife and his three amazing children. You can sign up for his newsletter and you can follow him on Twitter, Instagram, Facebook, Amazon, Threads, Bluesky, TikTok, and Goodreads.

Blaine Daigle

Having lived his entire life deep in the gut of Louisiana, Blaine Daigle grew up surrounded by ghost stories of haunted plantations and cursed woodlands. He still lives in Louisiana with his wife and two children and can't wait to pass on the nightmares to his kids..when they are old enough. During the day he teaches high school English. At night, he enjoys diving deep into the fears that shape and mold the world around him.

Eric Butler
Eric Butler was born in 1975 to a military family in Germany. He spent the majority of his formative years bouncing around Europe, the United States, and Central America before settling down in Texas. He is a fan of the horror genre but enjoys reading all kinds of fiction. He plans on mixing many of his favorite genres together in future works. He lives in the Dallas/Fort Worth area of Texas with his wife, son, and a stable of dogs and cats. He publishes under the Naked Cat Press brand, inspired by his sphynx Isis.

Tony Evans
Tony Evans is a crafter of horror and dark fiction, father, wildlife biologist, and member of the Horror Writers Association. Originally from the Appalachian foothills of eastern Kentucky, Tony grew up listening to stories of mountain monsters and holler witches, and his writing tends to reflect the culture and folk-tales of the area. While he sometimes enjoys what is termed 'quiet horror', Tony is much happier watching good old-fashioned slasher movies and reading about the boogeyman, demons, and anything else that may be hiding under the bed or in the closet.

His writing influences include: Stephen King, Neil Gaiman, Clive Barker, and Ray Bradbury, whose early work and short fiction leaves him wondering where 'true horror' has gone. He currently lives in Bardstown, Kentucky where he spends his time with his wife and two young daughters - his favorite little monsters.

Follow him on Twitter/Instagram: @tonyevanshorror

William F. Gray

William F. Gray is the best-selling author of THE DEVIL WITHIN US ALL, a small town horror novel inspired by the evil average people are capable of on an everyday basis. Taking cues from his own experience and the world at large, Gray creates horror that attempts to worm itself into your heart as well as your mind. His self-published debut THE MAN BEHIND THE DOOR tackles themes such as grief, trauma, and addiction through the lens of a ghost story, the main character of which is inspired by his own late father, while his latest effort OUR FATHERS' BURDEN is Appalachian horror that focuses on the stigma that still surrounds mental health issues, especially amongst men.

He currently lives in West Virginia with his wife, son, and daughter while working as a Lead Pharmacy Technician. His hobbies include reading, playing video games with his wife, and playing music.

Ashon Ruffins

Ashon Ruffins is an award winning author, native New Orleanian, and a Veteran. He holds a Master's in Business Administration, while holding certifications for several other professions. He loves the art of story telling in all genres and believes the best lessons in life can be told through fiction. The human struggles and victories are perfect avenues to tell outstanding stories through all genres. He simply loves spending time with his family or submerging himself in a good book or movie. Ashon is a huge mental health advocate.

K.K. Monroe

KK Monroe is a horror author, cognitive-linguistic specialist (by day), and an avid genre-fluid reader. She resides in Virginia with her husband and two pups. Firstborn American to immigrants who were raised under Tito's communist regime in former Yugoslavia; KK's unique bicultural upbringing has deep roots in oral storytelling traditions, dark Slavic Mythos, and cautionary folktales of a pagan-rich heritage. This cultural milieu shapes the lens of the author's writing style, evolving interests, and voice. In her free time, she enjoys tackling her TBR, watching scary movies, cooking ethnic foods, and falling down obscure rabbit holes in the name of research. Her short fiction has been published in Cosmic Horror Monthly and Screams from The Dark Ages. Her debut collection of quiet, cosmic horror "Things from the Dark" can be found on Amazon.

Timothy King

Timothy King is an adult horror author who enjoys delving into the complexities of human nature. When he is not writing spine-chilling tales, he is spending time with his wife and kids in beautiful Tampa, Florida.

Red Lagoe

Red Lagoe is the author of *Bloodstains by Gaslight*, *In Excess of Dark*, and three horror collections, including *Impulses of a Necrotic Heart*. In addition to writing, Red loves creating art through traditional fine art mediums, and she enjoys paddling through the cypress trees of coastal Virginia's bayou-esque waterways.

LM Kaplin

LM Kaplin is an author from upstate New York who has been a horror enthusiast in all forms his entire life. His morbid obsession with the macabre began one night while watching Poltergeist as a young child. The next morning, he began searching for ancient burial grounds in the backyard. Dismayed at not uncovering any evil spirits, he buried his own demons for future generations to find. It's time to start digging them up.

Heather Ann Larson

Heather Ann Larson is the editor of this anthology as well as its predecessors, Screams From The Ocean Floor, Screams From Beyond The Veil, and Screams From The Dark Ages as well as The Books of Horror Indie Brawl Anthology. She has also edited novels by authors Justin Boote, Sean McDonough, Timothy King, D.W. Hitz, LM Kaplin, and more. In her spare time, she... Who are we kidding? There is no spare time!!!

R.J. Joseph

R.. J. Joseph is an award winning, Shirley Jackson and Stoker Award™ nominated Texas based writer/speaker/editor. Her creative and academic work examines the intersections of race, gender, and class in the horror genre and popular culture. Her next short story collection, My Monsters Ain't like Yours, will be released in summer 2026 by Quill & Crow Publishing.

She occasionally peeks out on various social media platforms from behind @rjacksonjoseph or at www.rhondajacksonjoseph.com.

James Kaine
James Kaine is a bestselling author, publisher and filmmaker born and raised in Trenton, NJ. An active pro member of the Horror Writer's Association, he brings readers visceral, haunting tales of terror.

Ted Tally, Academy Award-winning screenwriter of The Silence of the Lambs and Red Dragon, called his book My Pet Werewolf "Twisty. Spooky. Shocking." and "Unputdownable."

BookLife by Publishers Weekly proclaimed his novel, The Dead Children's Playground, "will chill readers to the bone." The book, the first in his American Horrors anthology series, has been a #1 bestseller in U.S. Horror on Amazon and was the winner of the 2025 Books of Horror Indie Brawl. His works are being translated into multiple languages, bringing James's cinematic style of scary storytelling to a global audience.

He resides in Hamilton, NJ with his wife, Jessica, their two children and an energetic Boston Terrier. When he isn't writing he loves to read, travel, cook, watch movies and learn new skills.

Edmund Stone
Edmund Stone is a horror writer and part time boat captain living on the Ohio River. But mostly he lives in his head, where he derives a wealth of characters and strange ideas. He's even seen a few strange things crawling from the water. He lives with his wife, four dogs, and a plethora of cats.